MW00873765

Available
from Katy Regnery

a modern fairytale

The Vixen and the Vet
Never Let You Go
Ginger's Heart (coming soon!)

THE BLUEBERRY LANE SERIES

THE ENGLISH BROTHERS

Breaking Up with Barrett
Falling for Fitz
Anyone but Alex
Seduced by Stratton
Wild about Weston
Kiss Me Kate
Marrying Mr. English

THE WINSLOW BROTHERS

Bidding on Brooks
Proposing to Preston
Crazy about Cameron
Campaigning for Christopher

ALSO

Frosted, a novella
Playing for Love at Deep Haven
The Wedding Date, a Kindle Worlds novella

Frosted

❄ ❄ ❄ ❄ ❄

Katy Regnery

First Edition: January 2015
Second Edition: April 2015
Cover Design: Marianne Nowicki
Formatting: Cookie Lynn Publishing Services

Katy Regnery
Frosted : a novella / by Katy Regnery – 1st ed.
ISBN: 978-1503158641

Because it's never, ever too late to fall in love.

And with gratitude and love to
Jamie, Jennie, Kate, Susan & Veronica.

Rock. My. World.

Chapter 1

Grace Luff stood in front of the sliding glass doors of her hotel suite balcony, eyes narrow and jaw set as a mug of hot coffee warmed her hands. Just outside, two Adirondack chairs were covered in several inches of fresh snow, much like the expanse of lake beyond—white and cold, as far as her eyes could see.

She glanced down at the neatly stapled packet on top of a nearby end table that read: "Agenda: Silver Wings Singles Weekend—Day One." Chewing on her bottom lip briefly, she knocked the packet off the table and into the trash can with one slippered foot.

When Grace's children had arranged for her to attend the weekend retreat for mature singles at a resort in the beloved Adirondack mountains of her youth, she had balked before finally accepting their gift. But upon waking up this morning—the dubious "Day One" of said packet—she wished she'd just stayed at home.

She knew their intentions were good, but she bristled at the idea of needing the help of a "Singles Weekend" to meet a man. Surely she would meet someone the old-fashioned way—by accidentally bumping her cart into his at the supermarket, or standing behind him on line at Starbucks. Perhaps her running club would pair her with a good-looking older man for one of her morning jogs around the Central Park reservoir. Eventually she'd meet someone who didn't just see dollar signs when they looked at her, right?

The truth, however, was that meeting someone new was challenging. The large fortune left to her by her husband made Grace suspicious of the men she met. She was never sure if they liked her for her, or if they were just interested in her fortune, and she was weary of the guessing game that came with being the widow of the late Harold Luff. Calling the inn and changing her surname from Luff to Holden, her maiden name, had been the only way Grace finally felt comfortable attending the weekend...not that she didn't like being Grace Luff, or—more accurately—Mrs. Harold Edwin Luff III. She *had* liked it. Very much.

Though their marriage had not been romantic, it had been one of warmth and friendship, kindness and companionship. Grace had honored her vows to the very end, holding Harold's hand as he finally drifted away, after battling cancer for five long years. And Grace had mourned him with true—if unromantic—affection.

That said, her grieving process had been atypical—instead of taking quiet moments to remember good days and process the pain of her loss, Grace had almost immediately launched into a plan to build a new hospital wing at New York Central Hospital, managing every detail of its execution, right down to hand-picking the marvelous staff, all of whom she knew by name. When the Harold Edwin Luff III Cancer Research Wing was finally completed last month, it was Grace, flanked by her step-children, son, daughter and beloved grandchildren, who had cut the light blue ribbon and opened the doors to the state-of-the-art facility.

Although Grace felt a quiet satisfaction that she'd not only fulfilled Harold's dying wish for a treatment and care center, but overseen the project on her own, she had to admit that since the opening of the wing, she'd finally felt the impact of his loss.

Staying very busy with the project for three solid years had supplanted opportunities for loneliness. In the past few weeks, that had changed. Though her children, grandchildren and activities kept her busy, a bit of melancholy had intruded on her quiet thoughts lately, despite Grace's best attempts to ignore it.

She was no longer someone's wife, and she had no important projects with which to occupy her time and avoid contemplation of her future. The questions of "Who am I now?" and "What do I want?" hovered imminent and nagging over Grace's head.

Who am I now?

Well, prior to meeting Harold, she'd been a nice girl from a good family who'd received her bachelor's degree and become a grade school teacher at a small private school in Connecticut. She'd met Harold, a financial wizard and the single father of one of her most challenging students, at a parent-teacher conference in the fall of her first year teaching. Later, he told her that it was directness—she'd gently, but firmly, made it clear that Harold's son was sorely in need of parenting—paired with kind blue eyes that had led him to choose Grace for the job of stepmother.

Used to getting what he wanted, Harold had pursued her doggedly for several months, and they eventually became good friends. Even though Grace wasn't in love with Harold, she'd eventually relented and accepted his proposal. He was funny and kind, and his vast fortune could offer her a very comfortable and interesting life in Manhattan—and in exchange, Grace would help the busy widower raise his two rowdy, motherless boys.

And so, on one sunny, spring day, seven months after that fateful conference, Grace Holden, who was barely an adult herself, had become Mrs. Harold Edwin Luff III.

After thirty-one years of marriage, raising two stepchildren and bearing a son and daughter of her own, Grace felt eons away from the awkward, coltish twenty-two year old that Harold Luff had married. Over the years, she had settled comfortably into her role as Mrs. Harold Edwin Luff III, society matron. She was respected and well-liked. All four of her children were successful and well-adjusted. But, now that the children were grown and Harold was gone, did she want to go on being Mrs. Harold Edwin Luff III?

Something about recreating herself appealed to Grace and she yearned to rediscover the girl she'd been before meeting Harold—the girl who'd loved reading and teaching, who'd felt more connected to the country than the city, and preferred fresh air to stuffy fundraisers—and the idea of adding a new chapter to her life appealed to Grace. The problem was that she'd been Harold's wife for so long, she wasn't certain it was *possible* to be someone else. She simply didn't know how to start over.

What do I want?

That answer came so much more swiftly to Grace:

Warmth. Romance. Love.

Though she'd never articulated it to her friends, or even to her daughter, Adelaide, to whom she was very close, Grace longed for romantic love in her life. She would always cherish the friendship and partnership she'd shared with Harold, but he'd chosen her out of necessity, and she'd accepted him out of friendship. Theirs had been a contract, not a love affair. In the past three years, whenever Grace read a romance novel or watched a love story on TV, her yearning for passionate love would swirl up, so thick and strong, it would leave an uncomfortable lump in her throat. And yet…after a marriage that had spanned decades, a body that had borne two children, and a bank account that muddied the waters of a suitor's intent, Grace had no idea where to find what she so desperately wanted.

So she remained where she was: her identity in limbo, and her life increasingly lonesome. Grace's daughter, with her trademark sensitivity, had noticed.

"You seem down, Mom," said Adelaide at lunch last week.

"Not at all, dearest."

"Just a little?" asked her daughter, peeking at her mother over the rim of a Herend tea cup.

"Addy," Grace said, giving her a look. "I have my hands full with so many activities and commitments, I've no idea where the time goes. I have you and your brother...and Harold's boys, of course. Little Jillian and dear Edwin come every Wednesday afternoon for granny-time. Goodness, I don't have a moment to be...*down*."

It was a lie. Grace *was* feeling down, but admitting that she was devolving into some lackluster widow who passed the rest of her days being paired with other women at her jogging club, delivering cookies to the nurses at the hospital and attending book club meetings was too self-defeating to admit.

Adelaide had reached across the little dining table at the club and grasped her mother's fingers gently, lowering her voice, but keeping it firm. "Mom, it's no use denying it. I can see it. I can *feel* it."

Grace had withdrawn her fingers immediately, uncomfortable with such a public display.

"Feel what, exactly?"

"Your loneliness." Adelaide sighed, sliding her abandoned fingers back to her lap. "Daddy's been gone for three years. Isn't it time to..."

Grace felt her cheeks flush, so she purposely lifted her cup to take a leisurely sip of tea before looking up at her daughter with carefully blank eyes.

No stranger to her mother's sense of propriety, Adelaide's expression was compassionate and kind as she tried a different avenue, saying softly, "You and Daddy were…good friends."

"Yes, we were. The best."

"I know." Adelaide cleared her throat, holding her mother's eyes. "But I never sensed that you were…passionate about each other. You know, in love."

"Addy!" Grace warned her daughter, looking around quickly to be sure they weren't overheard.

Adelaide leaned forward, lowering her voice even further. "Mom, I don't mean any disrespect to Daddy or his memory. I loved him, too." She drew her bottom lip into her mouth and gulped softly before continuing, "But don't you—don't you *want* someone? Don't you want to *be* with someone?"

Another rush of blood heated Grace's cheeks, surely coloring them from pink to crimson as she looked down, reaching for her tea again. It was like Addy had some magical insight into her mother's mind, her observations were so astute.

Don't you want *someone?*

Yes, of course she did. But, where to begin? It was all too overwhelming. She didn't trust the men she met socially in New York and didn't know how to meet someone to whom she would be anonymous and new.

Instead of tackling the uncomfortable quandary, she backtracked the conversation to Harold. "Addy, your father and I had a very strong, respectful, um, stable—"

"Are you talking about a marriage or a business arrangement? Strong? Respectful? Stable?" When Grace looked up, a mildly exasperated Adelaide cocked her head to the side. "What about love, Mom? What about passion?"

Her daughter's eyes were soft and searching. Grace sighed.

Damn all those romantic movies we always watched together when she was little. I should have added more documentaries to the mix.

"For heaven's sake." Grace scoffed lightly. "I'm a *grandmother*."

"For heaven's sake, indeed," said Addy with a subtle eye roll. "You're only fifty-six. You're still young."

Grace stared at her daughter in surprise for a moment, her eyes filling with uncharacteristic moisture from Addy's sweet words. Oh, how good it felt to hear them. Despite her relatively-young age, during the years she had nursed Harold and even after, she hadn't felt very young at all. Hearing Addy say, *You're still young* was a balm, a blessing.

"Thank you dear, but I'm sure I'll meet—"

"I want to help." Adelaide's sweet face was slightly sheepish as her words came out in a whispered rush. "I know you might not—well, *love* my idea, but it's perfectly respectable and please just promise me you won't say no without thinking it over."

"Thinking over *what*, exactly?" asked Grace, her heart picking up speed.

Adelaide had lifted her purse from the floor and extracted a white envelope simply addressed "Mom." She placed it on the snowy white tablecloth between them and then slid it to her mother with a quick nod. Shrugging quickly into her coat, she stood up and leaned down near her mother's ear.

"Please go, Mom. It's all arranged," she whispered in Grace's ear. "Three years is long enough to grieve someone you weren't in love with."

"My life is not a rom-com, Adelaide," she said softly, glancing at the envelope without touching it.

"But it *could* be," murmured her daughter before kissing

her mother's cheek good-bye.

A frown pulled down the corners of her mouth as Grace took another sip of the weak, hotel-room coffee, still staring out at the frosted lake. Addy's gentle, but persistent hope and a misguided search for "could be" had somehow led Grace to The White Deer Inn…and now here she was, feeling irritated and disappointed and the weekend had barely begun.

In the week following their lunch, the envelope Addy had given Grace, which held a brochure about the singles weekend and a pre-paid voucher, had plagued her.

When Grace was paired up with another fifty-something widow for her Saturday morning run, the idea of going north to Deer Mountain had pestered her with every stride she took.

When her grocery cart didn't magically bump into the cart of an eligible, unknown, single man at the store on Tuesday, she heard Addy's words— *don't you want someone? Don't you want to be with someone?*—loud and strong in her ears.

When her good friends announced at book club on Wednesday that they'd found the perfect bachelor for Grace to meet, if she was willing to date "a very young eighty," she had finally dug the brochure out of her purse again.

And when she arrived at the hospital wing on Wednesday afternoon with cookies for the nurses, and ended up staying to comfort a recent widow, she swore that brochure finally grew hands that reached out and shook her. Hard.

But she was still dragging her feet until Thursday night when, damn it, she'd caught a late-night viewing of the classic Spencer Tracy-Katharine Hepburn movie, *Desk Set,* on TV.

For her whole life, Grace had felt a strong kinship to Katharine Hepburn—they both had reddish-brown hair, blue eyes and spare, athletic builds—and Grace spoke with that same clipped, outdated New England accent that had been a trademark of the famous actress. Like Hepburn, Grace had grown up on an estate in Connecticut surrounded by wealth and comfort, and at first glance, she had a similar no-nonsense demeanor. But it was even more than that. Back in the 70s, when Grace was still a teenager, Katharine Hepburn had given a late-night interview in which she shared, "I strike people as peculiar in some way, although I don't quite understand why. Of course, I have an angular face, an angular body and, I suppose, an angular personality, which jabs into people."

As a teen, Grace had stared at the TV, transfixed by these simple words. Sighing with self-awareness, she so closely identified with that description, both physically and emotionally, she'd spent the ensuing week researching Hepburn's life. Fascinated with the private relationship between Katharine Hepburn and Spencer Tracy, Grace had read everything possible about their clandestine, deeply devoted, love affair. In fact, reading every shred of information about *their* passion for one another was the closest Grace had ever come to a love affair of her own.

So, the night before last, swept away by the simple romance of the movie—a story of two fifty-somethings who find love late in the game—Grace had suddenly whipped the covers off her body, jumped out of bed and found herself packing her bags at one o'clock in the morning. Then, she had arranged for a car service to the airport before she could talk herself out of it and set her alarm for six o'clock.

Perhaps it was Addy's words about Grace never having known true, passionate love with her husband, or her assurances that it wasn't too late. Or maybe it was the fact that Grace's toes had curled when Kate got that smack on the lips from Spence at the end of the movie. Whatever the reason—and Grace had done her level best not to overthink it—she'd somehow found herself arriving at The Deer Mountain Inn yesterday afternoon...

...and regretted her impromptu decision by bedtime.

The resort itself was just as elegant as it had always been.

Her room was quite pleasant.

Told that there was an informal "Welcome Mixer" going on in the bar, Grace had dressed in a modest maroon wrap dress, put on her "Grace Holden" name badge and dutifully headed down to the bar/lounge...which was where her "Kate-Spence" fantasy had gone up in foul-smelling smoke. Cigar smoke, in fact. Lots of it.

Taking a sip of her coffee, Grace wrinkled her nose and huffed softly, thinking of last night: all those big-bosomed, autumn-aged ladies on the prowl and the handful of overconfident bachelors evaluating their possible conquests.

As Grace had fingered her pearls nervously, sipping a watered-down gin and tonic in a corner of the bar, she'd assessed the situation quickly: there were twice as many women attending the weekend as men, and scanning them, leaning confidently against the bar, not one made her heart go pitter-patter. They were stuffed and arrogant, smiling their "I'm a prize. I'm a prize. I'm *such* a prize." grins as their gazes swept the room, never lingering long on thin, angular Grace, who, at worst, probably looked unapproachably cool, and at best, blended into the shadows cast on the hard wooden wall of the little pub. For half an hour she'd stood in the corner and held her drink, feeling increasingly pathetic, while not one eligible silver wing of the male species approached her even to say hello.

Why this hurt so much, she didn't know. She told herself that she was a mature woman, established and respected at home in Manhattan—there was no good reason her confidence should be affected by a few shabby bachelors ignoring her. But her internal pep talk hadn't helped. The very sparse optimism with which she'd arrived at The White Deer Inn bid a hasty retreat and the longer she stood in the corner, ignored and alone, the more she wished she'd never come. Finally, after almost an hour of uncomfortable solitude, and with tears burning the backs of her eyes, she placed her half-finished drink on an empty cocktail table and headed back upstairs.

What she had realized, as her cheeks flushed with heat on the lonely elevator ride back up to her suite, was that the "Welcome Mixer" had been a test of sorts. A test of fate. She'd stupidly expected Spencer Tracy to sidle up beside her with some tart witticism—perhaps some mildly vulgar observation that would make her laugh, shock her, quietly delight her. A spark. A dash of wonder. The slightest sliver of surprise on the horizon of a ho-hum future.

But fate had failed her.

Without Harold's strong arm around her waist, she felt lost. The Silver Wings weekend was going to be full of desperate women more confident and forward than Grace, and men that would ignore her unless they discovered her real name—Mrs. Harold Edwin Luff III—at which point they'd suddenly vie for her company and find her fascinating.

She rolled her eyes and sniffed disgustedly.

Well, forget it.

As Grace finished her coffee, turning away from the blanket of white outside, she looked down at the trash can with satisfaction and firmly decided to avoid *all* Silver Wings events for the rest of today. Maybe by tomorrow she'd have the spirit to try again, but for now, she was done.

In the meantime, she'd spend some time enjoying the scenery and tranquility of The White Deer Inn, reading her book or bundling up for some fresh air. As a young girl, she'd spent several weeks every winter at the venerable old resort and she was anxious to explore the grounds through a mature lens. Still, she couldn't help the wave of gloom that washed over her...and told her just how much she'd hoped to end her streak of loneliness by meeting someone special this weekend.

She sighed as she headed toward her bedroom to get dressed. If a "future someone" existed for Grace, she felt quite certain he wasn't in attendance at the Silver Wings Singles Weekend. In fact, despite her quiet longing for a Hepburn-Tracy romance of her own, she worried that a "future someone" might not exist at all.

Chapter 2

Grace ducked into the small sundry store right off the lobby and purchased a cup of hot coffee and a pastry wrapped in plastic. Keeping her head down and sunglasses on, for fear of running into the overly-enthusiastic Silver Wings coordinator, she quickly headed out the sliding glass front doors of the main lodge, peeking up to see a sign that indicated the lake, boathouse and recreation center could be reached by following a path to the left, while the conference center and stables were to the right. Steering left, she decided to stroll by the lake with her breakfast and see if it was still possible to rent snowshoes or skis from the rec center as she had during childhood vacations.

Silver Wings be damned, she thought, feeling stronger and better with every step away from the lodge. She could still enjoy the austere, frosted beauty of the Adirondacks with an agenda of fresh air and exercise.

Grace's phone buzzed in her pocket. She balanced the half-eaten pastry on top of her coffee cup and answered the call.

"Hello?"

"Mom! You went! You're there!"

Grace felt her lips tilt up in a small grin. Addy's enthusiasm was infectious.

"Well…the room was paid for, after all. It would have been

wasteful to refuse. What choice did you leave me?"

"I'm so delighted! Well, I don't want to keep you from the…" Addy paused. "Wait a second. You're supposed to be at the Welcome Breakfast. How come it's so quiet?"

"Slipped away when my phone rang," lied Grace quickly. She didn't have the heart to tell Addy the Silver Wings part of the weekend was already a bust.

"Oh. Well…did anyone look *interesting*? Or *familiar*?"

"Familiar?" Grace's heat dropped. "Oh, Addy…what did you do?"

"This is unconfirmed," said her daughter, "but Stewart Whitman may or may not have also been invited to The White Deer Inn."

"Adelaide!" Grace stopped in her tracks, shaking her head with pique. "Please tell me you did *not* invite Stewart here this weekend."

"But you *like* him," said Addy sheepishly.

"As you well know, Stew and I are just friends. *Friends.* And that's all we'll ever be. He's almost eighty, for goodness sake!"

"So was daddy," protested Addy, "and Mr. Whitman is a very handsome older man."

"Addy, I have *no* romantic interest in Stewart. Zero." She sighed, knowing that marriage to Stewart would lead her to the same sort of respectful, passionless union she'd had with Harold, and that's not what Grace wanted. "It'll be very awkward to see him here. You've likely raised his expectations with this stunt."

"I'm sorry, Mom. I should have told you that Shannon invited Stewart."

Shannon Whitman, Stewart's daughter, was Addy's oldest and best friend, and Grace had felt the pressure of the girls' good intentions over the last year as Grace and Stewart were invited to parties, dinners and holiday events, always—and conspicuously—the only singles in attendance.

Grace took a deep breath and sighed again, resuming her walk toward the rec center. "Yes, you should have. But it's too late now."

"What will you do?"

"The ratio of women to men is in his favor," said Grace dryly. "I have no doubt he'll find someone nice."

"*You're* nice," said Addy. "*You* deserve someone nice, too."

"Well, don't ring the church bells just yet," she cautioned gently, thinking of the breakfast from which she was hiding. "Kiss the babies from granny, okay? Bye, dear."

Just as she was pulling the phone from her ear, she heard Addy's voice. "Mom? Mom?"

"I'm still here."

"I just wanted to say…keep your heart open, okay? You never know. I love you. Bye."

Keep your heart open.

Grace's eyes pricked with tears, suddenly, as she placed her phone back in the pocket of her down parka.

Keep your heart open.

It was such a sweet and simple piece of advice, and yet Grace didn't know how to actualize it. Had her heart been open to Harold all those years ago, or had she merely chosen him as a safe landing place?

Grace hadn't been a beautiful girl—she'd been gangly, small-chested and fit, her features more sharp than soft, with no lush curves to warm up a man at night. By twenty-two, Grace had been passed over more times than she could count—nobody's first choice date to homecoming or prom, no serious boyfriend in high school or college. When Harold showed such intense interest in her, she'd been flattered and a little relieved. She quickly convinced herself that there was tremendous value in a marriage based on mutual kindness, respectability, and friendship. He was in need, and she would be useful. It wasn't the sexiest basis for a marriage, but it was valid, wasn't it?

Of course Grace had wondered now and then over the years: What would it have been like to hold out for her soul-mate instead of marrying a friend in need? Would she have been alone forever? Or would she have eventually found the Spence to her Kate, someone for whom her heart would have opened like a flower?

Taking off her leather gloves, she swiped at her eyes. It was too late for recriminations. There was no sense in looking back. The only way possible, was forward.

Looking up from the snowy path, she recognized the log cabin-style building ahead with smoke billowing cheerfully from an ancient brick chimney. A large sign over the front door read "Recreation Center" in dark green and Grace's spirits were buoyed when she saw two young girls exit the building carrying skis. With any luck, there'd be some left for her too.

Keep your heart open.

The best Grace could promise was that she would try.

***

The young man behind the counter handed two pairs of skates to the teenagers in front of Grace. As they turned from the counter and took a seat on a nearby bench to lace up, she stepped forward.

"Well, good morning! I'm Roger! How can I help you, ma'am?" He had bright blue eyes and a cheerful smile on his young, handsome face.

"I thought I'd rent some cross country skis," she said, glancing at the price chart over his head. "I'm a hotel guest."

He rifled through a file under the counter and placed a slip of paper in front of her. "Alrighty! Just need your room number and your size."

He grinned as he said this, and Grace almost smiled back at his bouncy enthusiasm, but as a rule she didn't approve of this much emoting over ski rentals, so she restrained herself. "410. Eight and a half."

Roger's face contorted into a cringe and he sighed, shaking his head like he was about to let down the General who'd sent him on the mission that could win the war. "Oh, man. Oh, wow, I hate to tell you this, but...we don't do half sizes."

Confused by this dramatic delivery, she stared at him, dumbstruck for a moment before parroting, "No half sizes?"

He took her response for censure and shook his head, pursing his lips and sighing. "Gosh, I hate to let you down."

"I'll take a nine instead."

"Yes!" he exclaimed, beaming at her. "Terrific!"

His blond exuberance reminded her of a Golden Retriever puppy and she half expected him to vault the counter and lick her face. He didn't. He turned and yelled toward a back room, the door slightly ajar, "Hey Dad, you got those nines all fixed up? Nice lady here wantin' to rent 'em." He faced Grace again and winked—*winked!*—at her. "Someone broke the binding. My Dad's just fixing them. He can fix anything."

For heaven's sake, she thought, *what a fuss just to rent a pair of cross country skis.*

It was starting to feel like more trouble than it was worth. All she'd wanted to do was hide out from the other silver wings and get some fresh air. But they didn't have her size and what if the binding broke again when she was a mile from the hotel? Then what? She could feel her scowl starting as she stepped back from the counter. "Forget it. I can just..."

23

"Here we are."

Her voice tapered off as the door to the back room opened all the way and an older man, about her age, stepped into view.

And damn if Grace Holden Luff didn't *feel* her heart open as she lifted her gaze and slammed her eyes into his.

Like any other blue-blooded New Englander worth her salt, Grace prided herself on her sense of composure. Which is why—as her fingers slowly balled into fists until her nails were curled painfully into the skin of her palm—her face betrayed nothing.

His eyes were blue. Bright blue like the Caribbean Sea or the summer sky or the raspberry-flavored sno-cones they sold before the fireworks on the Fourth of July. A color blue that should be impossible in nature and yet there it was, in kind eyes fringed with dark lashes looking back at her from across a scuffed counter. He was solid and stocky, just about her height. His body was barrel-shaped, but fit, and his dark-blond hair was streaked with white, especially at the temples. His face wasn't wrinkled, but his laugh lines were deep, and he had the look of a man who'd lived a good portion of his life outdoors, soaking up the sun, welcoming the buffet of the wind against his cheeks.

"You the lady that needs the nines?" he asked, and she saw the father-son resemblance as his lips turned up into a grin, holding up the ski boots. "Binding was broken."

Her heart fluttered—*fluttered!*—as she watched his eyes crinkle with mischief.

You're a tease, aren't you? she thought, wondering how many hearts had fallen for that smile in his lifetime. She physically fought the impulse to step forward, closer to him. She had a sudden thought that he'd smell like leather and fresh air and pine and she wanted to find out if she was right.

For heaven's sake, Grace, you're behaving like a teenager!

Clearing her throat, she nodded at him.

"So I heard," she finally answered, her voice overly crisp, even in her own ears.

"Fixed it," he added as if she'd been warm instead of cool, and winking at her as his son had before.

Her heart kicked into a higher gear and she swallowed before taking a deep breath. She knew her cheeks had colored because she could feel the flush of heat and rush of blood.

"So I heard," she said again, softening her tone this time. She felt her lips wanting to tilt up, wanting to answer his, but she didn't let them. Overcome by her response to him, her first instinct was to flee the shop as quickly as possible…but where would she go? Back to the other silver wings? Oh, Lord, no.

"You know how to use 'em?" he asked, those blue eyes holding hers as he circled the counter.

"S-Skis? Of course."

He laughed good-naturedly. "We get some folks here who want to try them out for the first time, and I always warn 'em: It's a hell of a work out." His eyes flicked quickly down her body after he delivered this advice. His voice was a smidge lower and his eyes a trifle darker when he found her eyes and spoke again. "But I suspect *you'll* be fine."

Grace blinked, fingering one pearl earring nervously. Was it her imagination or had this ski shop manager just checked her out? Fearing her heart would thump right through her rib cage and flop onto the rental shop floor, she pressed her hands to her cheeks and sat down on the bench vacated by the skaters.

"I—I'll just, ah…"

Before she could catch her breath completely, he was kneeling at her feet, reaching for her rubber and leather snow boots, his gnarled, masculine hands surprisingly graceful as they opened her laces.

25

"I'm Tray, by the way," he said, then chuckled softly. "That rhymed."

Though he didn't look up from unlacing her boots, the tips of his ears turned pink, and Grace fisted her fingers because she had an overwhelming urge to reach out and touch them.

"Tray?" she asked. "That's unusual. I mean, for our generation. I don't recall a lot of Tray's."

He sighed, huffing softly, before looking up at her. "My real name is actually Tracy, which is just as bad as Sue." He grinned. "You like Johnny Cash?"

"I don't know," she answered honestly, her voice barely a murmur.

The whole earth had tilted on its axis when he told her his name. Her lips had parted, her eyes had widened, and she'd quickly stared down at her lap to hide her discomposure. His name was Tracy…*Tracy.*

His voice interrupted the wildness of her thoughts. "Never listened to him?"

"I don't believe so."

"That's a shame. He's one of the greats."

"Like Mozart?" she asked, raising her eyes to his.

He beamed at her like she'd just made a terrific joke. "Exactly! Like Mozart! Ha. You're a pip."

Never having been called a "pip" before, Grace found she liked it far more than she probably should, and bit the inside of her lip to keep from grinning. Still, she was fairly certain her eyes were twinkling because he winked at her again before pulling off one snow boot and then the other.

"So, I'm Tracy Bradshaw, called Tray. And you are…?"

Pip. *No.*

Kate. *No.*

"Grace."

"Grace," he whispered reverently. He tilted his neck back and looked up at her face, his blue eyes filled with wonder as he searched her eyes. "Like Grace Kelley. That's the prettiest name I ever heard. You know? I don't think I've ever met a Grace in real-life before."

"Now you have," she answered, and without giving them permission, her lips tilted up into a smile.

His smile widened as his warm hand clamped around her socked ankle and guided her foot into the first ski boot. "Now I have."

Chapter 3

Tray had offered to send Roger with her, but Grace had declined
the services of a tour guide, feeling an intense need to
unscramble her head by taking deep gulps of fresh, mountain air
and talking herself out an unsuitable attraction that had rocked
her fifty-six year old body like a bolt of lightning.

"I'd offer to take you myself," Tray had said, his face
pursing with regret, "but I have a meeting with the resort
manager in an hour. I can assure you that no one knows the trails
like Roger, here."

"I'll be fine," Grace had insisted, her heart leaping a little
from his words.

"I hope so." He'd grimaced a little, opening the door of the
rental shop and looking up at the sky. "I don't like the way it's
looking, Grace. Too much cloud cover."

Grace had taken her phone out of her parka pocket and
checked the weather. "It says it's going to clear up by noon."

His eyes had darted to the phone. "Do me a favor and put
my number in there? If anything happens…anything—you get
stuck, you get tired, you name it—you call me and I'll come get
you or send Roger, okay?"

She'd stared back at him, boiling down his entire message
to: *I want to give you my phone number.* When she didn't

answer, he'd tugged the phone from her hands and programmed his number in himself, then handed it back to her, still warm from his hands. She'd clasped it against her chest, rather than dropping it back into her pocket. "Okay."

He scanned her body slowly, then, from the pom-pommed black angora hat on her head to her black parka and leather gloves, to her blue jeans, stuffed into cross country boots. "You look real good, Grace. Ready to go, I guess."

She squelched the slight whimper that threatened to break free from the back of her throat and grabbed the skis and poles Roger was holding out for her.

"I'm off, then!" she'd chirped, turning her back to them and quickly exiting the shop.

And now here she was…a couple of miles from the rec center, all alone, trying to make sense of what had just happened between her and Tracy Bradshaw. She planted her sticks and slid forward, again and again, a sheen of sweat covering her brow.

While part of her was desperate to believe that Mr. Bradshaw had been flirting with her, a louder, more sensible part of Grace insisted that his job was to work with wealthy resort guests, and he was expected to be amenable and charming to *all* of them. Right? Right.

Plant pole, slide. Plant pole, slide.

It wasn't his fault that he was an exceptionally good-looking man—the sort of man who made a sensible woman's mind wander. A little short, maybe, but his body was a tight package of muscle, obviously no stranger to hard work and lots of exercise. His eyes were utterly captivating and when he smiled, those laugh lines testified to decades of good humor.

Though she'd checked out his ring finger covertly several times, there wasn't a ring, indentation or a tan line, and she wondered about Roger's mother. Surely there had been a Mrs.

Bradshaw at some point? But not for some time, Grace guessed. It had taken her over a year to part with her own wedding ring, and another to lose the tan line and indentation. If he'd ever worn one, she guessed it was at least two or three years ago.

And a man like that almost certainly has a girlfriend, she told herself, suddenly thrusting her poles a little too deep into the snow and having to yank them back out. He fairly reeked of virility—a man like that wasn't spending his nights alone. Oh, no. He'd have some local woman in his bed…a masseuse who worked in the hotel spa perhaps, or the concierge at the reception desk. Grace had noticed an attractive woman about her age when she checked in—it was completely possible she was Mr. Bradshaw's paramour.

Her eyes narrowed and she compensated for her envy of this charmed concierge by increasing her pace. Plant, slide, plant, slide, plant slide.

"It's none…of your business…with whom…Mr. Bradshaw…spends his time," she panted.

She was here for some exercise and to enjoy the bounty of nature, and anyway, she'd be gone the day after tomorrow. The upshot of the situation, she tried to convince herself, was that meeting Mr. Bradshaw had proven that Grace wasn't too old to feel the sharp pang of desire, but her renewed spirits were short-lived as her mind settled on a troubling thought. Her throat tightened a little when she thought about her fifty-six year old body. She had always been fit, which meant she wasn't in bad shape for her age, but almost six decades of wear and tear had left stretch marks, wrinkles, sun spots and the odd varicose vein. The only man who'd ever looked upon her small breasts and soft belly had been Harold, and truth be told, there hadn't been a lot of looking—mostly just fumbles in the dark, under the covers, without much looking at all.

Grace bit her lip as she wondered, just for a moment, what it would be like to *be* with Mr. Bradshaw—to be clasped against his muscular body, to feel the heat of his skin pressing into hers. *He* would look at her. He would insist. She felt it in her bones. He'd want to *see* everything. Her breathing hitched and her cheeks flamed. She certainly wasn't ready for anything like that. Was she? No, she wasn't. Absolutely not. Absolutely, positively not.

A drop of sweat plunked from her forehead to her lip and she paused her skis, licking the saltiness away with her tongue, and looking ahead. So consumed with her thoughts, she wasn't completely sure where she was now, but at some point she'd left the marked trail. Looking to her right, she saw the mountain she'd stared at this morning from her hotel window, and to her left was a vast, snow-covered field. Or lake. She couldn't be sure, but it was flat and covered in snow.

Buzz buzz. Buzz buzz.

The phone in her pocket was buzzing and her heart hammered, wondering if it was Mr. Bradshaw checking up on her. She pulled off a glove with her teeth and grabbed the phone from her pocket, her breath catching to see the name "The White Deer Inn" pop up in the Caller ID box.

"Hello," she said breathlessly.

"Ah! Mrs. Holden?"

Her face fell when she heard a woman's perky voice on the other side of the line, and for a moment she was perplexed. Was this woman looking for Grace's deceased mother? It took her a moment to remember that she'd given her maiden name when she checked-in at the hotel.

"Hello, there. Is this Mrs. Holden?"

"Yes. Yes, this is Grace Holden."

"This is Marissa Meyers, the coordinator for the Silver

Wings weekend."

Grace grimaced. "Mm-hm. Yes."

"We missed you at breakfast and I noted you also missed the scavenger hunt this morning."

Grace was silent. She was fifty-six years old. She was worth almost twenty million dollars. She'd raised four children and buried a husband. She refused to answer to a resort activity coordinator, or account for her time to anyone.

Miss Meyers continued sheepishly. "Well, I, um, I wanted to be sure everything was okay."

"Yes," answered Grace. "I decided to do a little skiing this morning."

"Oh. Oh, well that's...wonderful. I wish I'd known. I could have paired you up with one of our bachelors."

Grace wrinkled her nose.

"Mrs. Holden?"

"You needn't worry about me, dear."

"Oh, I know. I just want you to—"

"I'm perfectly fine, Miss Meyers," she said, adding a little steel to her voice.

"Of course." Miss Meyers paused and Grace could tell she was mustering her courage for another line of attack. "Will you be back for lunch?"

Grace looked up at the clouds that had still not cleared into blue sky. She didn't know how much longer it would be wise to stay out here in the cold, quiet wilderness of Deer Mountain. Still, she wasn't anxious to join the planned activities either. "I have no idea."

"But surely you'll be back for dinner?"

"If I am, Miss Meyers, it'll be—"

Miss Meyes interrupted her in a rush. "It's just that a Stewart Whitman saw your name badge, and he asked me if you were actually Grace Luff. I checked your credit card receipt and realized you were. Mr. Whitman is quite anxious to see you, to spend time with you…and I just—well, I hoped I could arrange a dinner reservation for the two of you!"

Grace took a deep breath.

Stewart Whitman on the prowl.

Oh, dear.

How awkward.

Grace and Harold had known Candace and Stewart Whitman for the better part of thirty years. Same country club in the Hamptons. Same church in the city. They attended many of the same charity events and had even vacationed together once or twice—once to Ireland for some golf, and once to Monaco for some sun. When Candace died last year, Grace had spent the day of her funeral organizing Stew's refrigerator with casseroles, and helping him receive his guests. He was a dear, old friend, and she'd been glad to lend a hand.

And—with Adelaide and Shannon's misguided assistance, no doubt—Stew had certainly been in touch this year. He'd called one time to offer his help with the hospital wing and another time to see if he could escort her to the annual Met gala. Grace had thought the calls awkward and rushed to get off the phone, anxious not to appear too indifferent, but even more careful not to appear too interested.

There was no way she could *refuse* dinner with such an old friend, but she feared that he'd been coached by the girls to make an overture toward Grace this weekend. She sighed loudly, rolling her eyes at such an unwelcome scenario. While Stewart would be an eminently *appropriate* choice of husband for Grace, she felt nothing but friendship for the tall, elegant widower several years her senior. She simply wasn't interested.

Mr. Bradshaw's eyes flitted quickly through her mind and

her stomach fluttered unexpectedly. The difference in the way she felt thinking of the two men was so vast and so visceral, it surprised her, but it was in no way ambiguous.

"Of course," said Grace evenly. "Stewart is a very dear, old friend. I'm happy to keep him company if you can't find a more *available* companion for him."

"Available?" asked Miss Meyers.

"Stewart and I are just *friends*," she said meaningfully, "as I mentioned."

"Oh, well," Miss Meyers answered enthusiastically, undeterred by Grace's discreet warning. "Friends is an excellent place to start, isn't it? Eight? In the Sycamore Room?"

Grace sighed. She hoped that Stewart would somehow sense her feelings and refrain from making an old friendship more awkward. Unlikely. Subtlety had never been his strong suit.

"Fine," said Grace, unenthusiastically.

"I'll take care of everything! Have a lovely ski!"

Grace took a deep breath and grumbled, letting her phone plop back into her pocket, and tugging her glove back onto her hand. No matter what their meddling brood of children thought, Stewart and Grace weren't a match.

She'd started the day believing that a "future someone" didn't exist at all, and she wasn't much more encouraged now. However, one vital, fundamental change in Grace's worldview since this morning, was that if there ever was a "future someone," she wouldn't settle for comfort. She'd settle for nothing less than passion, like Hepburn and...Tracy.

Tracy.

There was no one to see, so when her lips trembled before sliding into a smile, she didn't bite her lip or cast her eyes down. She let them widen and part, until her gleaming teeth were bared and her cheeks ached from grinning.

"I won't settle again," she whispered fiercely, feeling the sanctity of the words, the certainty of them, the blessed relief of the promise she was making to herself. As Addy had observed, Grace still had thirty or forty years left, and she would rather live them alone than live in passionless companionship.

"Sorry, Stew," she said softly, turning around to start retracing her tracks back to the rec center. "But dinner will *just* be dinner, I'm afraid."

As she maneuvered back around, she noticed it: the first heavy flakes falling to the ground around her. Plop! One landed on her shoulder. Another on her hat. It was snowing. And it was starting strong.

Snow? She grimaced, sliding her skis into her tracks and swooshing forward. She hadn't seen snow in the weather forecast at all. Planting her pole with a new sense of urgency, she set off at a steady pace. She estimated that she'd skied for over an hour when she'd gotten the phone call from Miss Meyers. It would take *at least* an hour to get back to the Recreation Center, even if she could maintain this speed, which she couldn't, because she was already starting to feel tired.

As the snow whipped into her face, coming down harder, she wished she'd worn a scarf, but the day had seemed mild this morning, she thought she'd be fine with a coat, hat and gloves. After fifteen minutes of hard skiing, she leaned against a tree, breathless and starting to feel genuinely worried. She could still make out her tracks for now, but just barely, and she wasn't even back to the main trail yet. At the rate the snow was falling, she feared the tracks would be covered soon.

Considering a call to Mr. Bradshaw, she decided instead to push forward. Once she found the main trail, she'd be fine, right? She'd just go slowly, following the trail markers until she found herself back at the resort.

Plant, slide. Plant, slide. Plant, slide, skid, fall. *Ouch!*

She felt her left ankle twist inside the boot before the sensation sluiced up her leg in a bolt of hot, white pain. Her ski hadn't released when she tripped, and when it nosedived into the snow, her ankle had turned.

She lay stunned and breathless, sprawled in the snow for a moment before shaking her head and forcing herself to sit up as best she could.

"Oh, God!" she yelped, feeling the wet snow seep through the back of her jeans as she reached forward to release the binding. She pressed hard. Nothing. She pressed again. Nothing. Her twisted ankle was trapped and she couldn't release the boot.

Reaching forward, she took the ski between her hands and righted it, wincing with pain as her ankle twisted back into a more natural position. She gasped and bit her lip, knowing that the ankle was going to start swelling in the tight boot. Her breathing quickened as the snow blew into her face and her butt felt increasingly wet and cold.

Rolling to her side, she lined up her skis and used her poles to push off, but it took several tries to stand upright, as her left ankle could barely hold her weight. She whimpered, feeling hot tears sliding down her now-cold cheeks, and used all of her strength to force herself up.

"Oh, my God!" she panted, gasping with pain as she shifted her body weight to her right side. The throbbing on her left side was so acute, her mouth watered and she felt her stomach threatening to revolt. Hot tears slid down her cheeks and she tried to find equilibrium, but the pain was so sharp, she feared falling again. Willing herself not to panic, she wound the pole strings around her wrists, hopped to a nearby tree, and leaned against it, catching her breath before pulling her phone

from her pocket. She had used all of her strength to get to the tree—there was no way she was going to be able to ski or walk back to the Recreation Center.

Grateful for an Edge signal, she had just started to dial Mr. Bradshaw's number when the sound of a motor broke through the white noise of snow and wind. It was coming closer and closer in fits and stops, as though the driver was following an uncertain path, unsure of where to go. As it got closer, she heard someone calling her name, "Grace! Grace? Grace!"

"I'm here!" she screamed, hopping to rotate her body around the tree and shout in the direction of the motor. It cut for a moment, and she screamed again. "I'm here! I'm here! Help!"

The motor revved up again, and a moment later, she saw Mr. Bradshaw cut through the snow on a snowmobile, headed right for her.

Never—no, not ever in the entire course of her entire life— had Grace been so happy to see someone.

Chapter 4

He pulled up beside her, his blue eyes at once worried and relieved as he hopped off the snowmobile and approached her with purposeful strides. When she didn't move toward him, his eyes dropped to her legs, focusing on her left leg, which she held slightly bent and an inch off the ground.

"What happened?" he asked, finally reaching her. He pulled off his gloves and cupped her cheeks with his warm, bare hands, looking into her eyes, searching her face. "Are you okay?"

Her lips parted in surprise and for a moment all of the pain in her left side momentarily vanished as she registered how tenderly he was touching her. Her words were breathless. "I—I twisted my ankle."

He winced, dropping his hands and squatting down in front of her. He released the right ski, then reached for the left binding and tried to release the ski, but it wouldn't budge.

"God damn it," he hissed, trying again. "This is my fault. I thought I had fixed it."

Every time he tried to release the binding, it jostled the boot and made fresh tears well in her eyes. She whimpered softly and his face whipped up. "I'm hurting you?"

"N-No. Yes," she sobbed, leaning back against the tree and

pulling her bottom lip into her mouth. "Please just get it off."

"Wait here."

He took her loose ski and sprinted over to the snowmobile, leaning it against the small vehicle. Opening a side compartment, he took out a screwdriver and ran back to her.

"Brace yourself," he cautioned, then knelt down and jammed the screwdriver into the binding. With a soft click, it finally released.

Grace ignored the darts of pain shooting mercilessly up her leg as Tray took the second ski back to the snowmobile, cursing under his breath. When returned to her, his face was worried, but determined.

"Put your arms around my neck," he ordered when he got close.

Her eyes widened. "I'm sure I can hop over to—"

He didn't let her finish. He took her wrists in his hands and pulled them around his neck, her poles hitting his back as they drooped over the edges of her gloves. Without saying another word, he lifted her into his arms, then turned back toward the snowmobile.

Grace had two thoughts:

One, *I'm in Mr. Bradshaw's—no, Tray's arms.*

Two, *he smells like fresh air, leather and pine, just as I knew he would.*

Resisting the urge to snuggle closer to the patch of exposed skin on the side of his neck which peeked out between his scarf and hat, her heart beat a primal rhythm as he carried her effortlessly over to the snowmobile. To her immense disappointment, it ended all too soon.

"Spread your legs," he barked through the whipping wind.

Her breath caught from the unintentional eroticism of the demand, but she spread them in time to be deposited unceremoniously onto the back of the snowmobile. Working quickly, he removed the poles from her wrists, picked up the skis and fastened her equipment to the back of the vehicle with a bungee cord. Climbing onto the snowmobile in front of her, he turned his neck, leaning back to place his lips as close as possible to her ear.

"Wrap your arms around my waist and hold on. It's coming down too hard to get back to the rec center. We'll go to the West Mountain Warming Hut until it clears up. There's a first aid kit there. You ready?"

"Yes!" she said, reaching around him and clasping her hands together around his chest. She could feel the rock hard expanse of muscle beneath her hands, and without thinking, she leaned forward and laid her cheek against his back as he turned over the engine and started off through the woods.

With his back as a shield, Grace was finally spared the constant bite of snow against her cheeks and she closed her eyes. Despite the sharp pain in her ankle, she took a deep, calming breath for the first time since she hung up with Miss Meyers, terribly grateful for the timely arrival and solid strength of her rescuer.

***

Ten minutes later, Tray pulled up in front of a small log cabin with a dark green sign that read "West Mountain Warming Hut." The snow was falling so thick by then, Grace was impressed that he'd been able to find the small building at all.

He cut the motor and threw his leg over the snowmobile to stand up. Cupping his hands on either side of her ear, he yelled, "Stay here for a minute. I'll be right back to help you."

When he leaned back, his fingers moved to the zipper of his coat, and before Grace could protest, he unzipped it and shrugged out of it, throwing it over her shoulders and pulling it together under her chin. It was heavenly warm and her eyes fluttered closed from the clean, masculine smell.

He fussed with the side compartment of the snowmobile beside her hip for a moment, finally pulling out a long cord with several jangling keys. Walking to the door, she watched as he tried one after the other in an attempt to unlock the door. Thank goodness the sixth or seventh key worked, and he pushed open the door of the little log building.

Turning back around, he returned to her and without him having to ask, she roped her arms around his neck so he could lift her from the snowmobile and carry her into the hut. It took her eyes a moment to adjust to the paucity of light, but she gradually made out a leather couch facing a massive flagstone fireplace in the center of the small room. To her left was a bank of windows with two or three bistro tables with two chairs at each, and to her right was a kitchen or snack bar area flanked by two doors. There was no light other than the white of the snow outside through the windows, no lights and no hum of electricity. It was a spare, tight space, but nothing had ever looked so inviting in all her life. Tray walked around the sofa, gently depositing her on it before going back to shut the door.

"I'll get it warmed up in here."

"Please take your coat back," said Grace, pulling it from around her shoulders.

"No, Grace." His hand landed on hers, gently stopping her. "I'm so angry with myself, I could punch something. I should've checked that binding again before letting you go. Instead I got…well, distracted. Please keep the coat until I get a fire going."

With an angry, sorry expression still darkening his handsome face, he turned away from her, taking logs and newspaper from a large pile beside the fireplace and fashioning a fire in the grate. A few minutes later, a cheerful blaze snapped and crackled before them. The instant warmth was welcome. Grace's ankle, however, was aching fiercely. She sat up straighter and reached down to unbuckle the boots.

"Let me do it," said Tray, kneeling beside the couch and unsnapping them open. He pulled the right boot off, setting it against the couch beside him, before looking up at her. "I'll go slow, okay?"

She winced, but nodded.

He reached into the left boot and pulled the tongue out as far as it would go then gripped her leg carefully before tugging.

Grace whimpered softly, clenching her eyes and gasping from the pain.

"Should I stop?" he asked, cringing with worry.

"Pull it off!" she sobbed. "Please."

She gritted her teeth as he gave the boot a good yank, falling backward as her foot finally slid free. It took Grace a moment to process the searing pain and open her eyes again. When she did, she could immediately see the difference between her two ankles. Even under two layers of socks the left one was considerably bigger.

Tray reached for her hand, which was gripping the edge of the leather couch like a claw, and squeezed it gently. "Hold tight, Grace. Let me get the first aid kit. Least I can do is find some Advil for the pain and wrap it up for you."

"Thanks," she said softly, willing herself not to cry. He already felt so bad, she couldn't bear to do anything that would make him feel worse.

Crossing in front of the dormant snack bar area, he entered the left door and Grace craned her neck to see where he'd gone. From her position against the side of the couch, she could make out a crowded, disorderly office: a desk that held a radio, files and a messy, faded bulletin board. A large first aid kit hung on the wall beside the board and there were two windows over the desk that looked like they were painted white, the snow still fell so thick and even outside.

Tray returned a moment later holding the first aid kit. Kneeling down beside her on the floor, he grimaced at her foot.

"I bet it hurts."

"It does," she said. "But at least I'm not trapped in the snow anymore. Thank you for coming when you did."

"Of course. I was worried the second you left. I could smell the snow coming."

"Smell it?"

"When you've lived in the mountains for as long as I have, you've got a sixth sense about snow. I don't even listen to the forecast anymore." He opened the kit and rustled around for an Ace bandage, holding it up and letting it unfurl onto the floor. "I'm going to take your sock off."

Her cheeks felt hot, and despite the pain in her ankle and the warmth of the fire, the flush was born of a different heat source altogether. She took a deep breath as his fingers pushed up the cuff of her wet jeans.

"What is this place?" she asked, trying to distract herself from his touch.

"Warming hut for skiers," he answered, focused on his work. "Your jeans are soaked."

"Why isn't it open today?"

He ignored her question. "You should take them off and dry them by the fire."

Wait. "What?"

"Your jeans. They're wet and freezing. You need to get them off."

Take off my pants?

43

She blinked at him. "Really, Mr. Bradsh—"

"Grace?" His face was serious when he looked up at her. No trace of teasing. "We're going to be here a while. That snow's not fixing to let up for another few hours and even then I'll have to dig out the snowmobile. It could take almost an hour to get back down the mountain and it'll be cold and dark. You'll need warm, dry pants." His face softened. "I have no designs on you, ma'am. I just want you to be safe and warm."

His words were respectful and polite.

I have no designs on you.

Her heart absolutely plummeted.

She straightened her back as best she could, raised her chin and gave him her well-practiced, frostiest look. "Thank you for your concern, but I'll be fine."

"No, you won't be."

Grace was unaccustomed to contradiction and her eyes blazed as she quickly retorted, "I assure you I will be completel—"

Holding up a hand to stop her, he shook his head back and forth, and sighed, as though losing patience with a petulant child. "Grace? Take off the jeans."

Standing up, he headed for an old-fashioned wooden trunk on the other side of the fireplace and flipped it open, removing a plaid wool blanket and placing it beside her thigh on the couch.

"You can cover up with this. I'll turn my back."

Standing only a foot or two away, he turned from her and faced the fire while Grace eyed the blanket, wrinkling her nose and furrowing her brows. She was trapped in a small cabin, on a mountain, in the middle of a snowstorm with a man she barely knew to whom she was wildly attracted, who—apparently—did not return the compliment. Now she was supposed to get half naked? She pulled her bottom lip between her teeth, and looked

44

up, her eyes smacking straight into Tray's tight bum in black snow pants.

I have no designs on you.

Angrily, she pulled his coat from around her and shrugged out of her own, throwing both onto the floor in a fit of temper. She dropped her fingers to the button of her jeans, unsnapping and unzipping them quickly and doing her best to shuck them down her legs. She sat up, pulling off the right leg, but winced as the left leg, which was wet and unwieldy, got caught on her ankle.

She whimpered softly, tugging at the wet denim.

"Need help?" he asked, still facing away.

From you, *Mr. No Designs?*

"Absolutely not."

Her hurt feelings somehow made it easier for her to ignore the pain as she yanked the jeans off and she threw them on the floor beside the couch. Settling back against the side, with her legs straight out in front of her, she unfolded the scratchy wool blanket and tugged it over her body, primly tucking it in on either side of her waist and under her legs so she looked like a plaid mummy from the waist down.

"All set?' he asked.

"Yes," she answered.

She knew she was weak for looking up at him as he turned around, but she couldn't help it. He'd wounded her pride when he told her he wasn't interested in her. Not that he was an appropriate choice for her on any level—he was the manager of a resort ski shop, for heaven's sake, and she was Mrs. Harold Edwin Luff III, millionaire widow from Manhattan. It's just that it had been so long—forever, truthfully—since any man had really and truly captured her interest, made her heart beat faster or her breath catch or her smile come out to play. It had felt so

lovely to want, to wonder if he wanted her, to breathlessly
wonder at the possibility of *something* simmering between them.
Crushing her feelings with his disinterest made her feel foolish
and undesirable.

Which is why the look in his eyes surprised her so much
when her eyes slammed into his.

His bright blue eyes were dark and he was clenching his
jaw when he turned to face her. For just a moment, his eyes
trailed from her face to her Nordic light blue and cream sweater
down to the blanket and back again.

You lied, she thought, surprised by how easy it was to
recognize hunger in a man's eyes when she'd rarely seen it
directed at her. It made her heart hammer against her ribs, and
her hand fluttered to flatten against her chest as her lips parted.
His eyes were focused on hers with irritation, yes, but they were
also wide and fierce as they stared back at her. He swallowed
and she watched his Adam's Apple bob before cutting her eyes
back up to his face.

"I won't," he said softly, then flinched, like he hadn't
meant to actually say the words aloud.

"You won't *what*?" she whispered, her tongue darting out
to wet her suddenly-parched lips.

"You're a stunning woman," he murmured, reaching down
to grab her jeans before turning away from her.

Never in her entire life had a man uttered such words to
her.

You're a—smart, clever, driven, sensible, focused—
woman? Sure. Stunning? Never. A fickle part of her heart,
desperate to believe him, made a mewling plea for her to accept
and own his words, but the larger part of her drowned out that
tiny voice with suspicion. She knew who she was: angular,
awkward, austere Grace. There was only one reason a man

would offer such a bold, outlandish lie. Only one, and it both skewered and hardened her heart that such a lie had been delivered by Tracy Bradshaw.

"No, I'm not," she answered, keeping her voice cool and level. "But I *am* very rich."

He was draping her jeans over the fireplace grate as she said this, and when he turned to her, his face backlit by the orange flames leaping and spitting behind him, he looked furious.

"How nice for you," he said.

She lifted her chin. "How nice for the man who marries me."

His lips dropped open and he put his hands on his hips, shaking his head back and forth with a look of shock and disappointment before closing his mouth and clenching his jaw. His eyes, searing and disturbed, scanned her face with severity and even though she felt completely naked, her pride demanded that she not look away.

"I take it back," he finally said in a low, curt tone.

"What?"

"How *awful* for you," he whispered with feeling, his forehead deeply creased.

She blinked. "What does *that* mean?"

"Do I think you're stunning? Yes, I do. Honest to God, on the head of my son, I do. Do I think you're interesting? You're a little prickly, but that just makes me more curious." He took a step toward her, his blue eyes boring into hers. "Do I give a rat's ass how much money you have in the bank? I do not. My own bank account is plenty comfortable, thank you very much." He clenched his jaw, staring at her in a way that made her very *un*comfortable, even though she couldn't imagine looking away. "How *awful* for you that a man can't give you an honest

47

compliment without you suspecting he has ulterior motives. How exhausting. How unbelievably—"

"That's quite enough," Grace said firmly, reaching up to wipe away the tear that was snaking down her cheek. "Quite, quite enough."

Chapter 5

Her pants had been draped before the fire for an hour now, and
her phone battery was almost dead. It didn't matter. Her signal
wasn't very strong or reliable with the storm raging outside. She
was able to retrieve an e-mail from Addy, apologizing again for
playing matchmaker, and wishing her a wonderful weekend.
There were several others from friends and two from the
hospital, asking if she'd chair the Annual Spring Ball. But New
York seemed a million miles away from her nest on a couch in
the middle of the woods during a flash blizzard. She set the
phone on the rustic coffee table in front of the sofa and pulled
the slipping blanket up a little to better cover herself.

After their very awkward exchange, Mr. Bradshaw had
taken off her sock and bandaged up her ankle without a word,
without looking at her, and Grace had endured his stoicism with
her own quiet discontent. He'd handed her two Advil without
making eye contact and found an unopened can of Root Beer in
the snack bar cabinet and placed it on the table within reaching
distance. Then he'd retired to the little office, drawing the line
between "the guest" and "the help" without uttering a word.

Every twenty minutes or so, he'd come out and poke at the
fire, adding another log, but he didn't look at her or say
anything, and as the minutes ticked by with the snow still

gusting outside, she felt worse and worse about the way she'd treated him, how she'd inadvertently accused him of complimenting her only to charm his way into her wallet.

If she was wary, it was only because she had reason.

A year after Harold had died, the unexpected and unwanted attention had surprised Grace: widower friends of her late husband, single brothers and cousins of her friends, an aging actor and a respected politician…all had pursued Grace at one time or another. They were—all of them—after her fortune, and Grace knew this because she wasn't beautiful, she had little in common with most of them and actual chemistry with none. They simpered and smirked at her, carefully agreeing with her at every turn and making it seem as though her interests were also their own. She'd only met one or two eligible, genuinely nice bachelors, who could have slipped into Harold's place very easily. One, in fact, was Stewart Whitman, with whom Grace could probably have spent many respectful, companionable years. And maybe she would have accepted Stewart eventually if she'd never come to The White Deer Inn and never come face-to-face with Tracy Bradshaw.

Yet here she was, *trapped* in a cabin with said Tracy Bradshaw, who had impacted her life so astonishingly in the course of a few short hours. A burly ski shop manager who carried her in his arms like she weighed nothing and bossed her around like no one had ever dared. A man with sno-cone colored eyes and deep laugh lines. A man she barely knew, but to whom she was drawn, nonetheless. So, why was she pushing him away with all her might?

He's simply not an appropriate choice for you, she reasoned.

A mountain man from upstate New York and a rich widow from Manhattan? It was absurd. They couldn't possibly be a match. But, after all, she wasn't husband-hunting here in the woods with Tracy Bradshaw, was she? No. This was just an unaccountable twist of fate. Couldn't she loosen up enough to enjoy him for a few hours? Couldn't she let her heart and belly flutter in that hot, delicious way she thought she'd never experience? Couldn't she allow herself the excitement of his company so that she'd recognize these feelings again if she ever happened to meet her "future someone"?

For heaven's sake, Grace, she thought. *Get out of your own way and enjoy him!*

Every moment that they shared the compact space without speaking felt like a wasted opportunity and finally she couldn't stand it anymore. A quick vision of Tracy kissing Hepburn popped into her head as he stalked back into the room to tend the fire, and she heard the words tumble out of her mouth,

"Tray. I'm sorry."

It was the first time she'd used his first name, and it felt significant somehow, to hear it in her own voice, in her own ears. It felt like she was crossing over from *there* to *here*, from the *past* to the *present*, from the *shadows* of yesterday to…well, to *now*.

His back stiffened and she watched as he slowly replaced the poker and turned to her.

His face was hard and internally Grace owned up to the fact that she'd accused him of something pretty odious. He deserved a proper apology. "Since my husband's death I've had some unwelcome attention because of the estate he left to me. I think I've become suspicious. But you didn't deserve that. Not at all."

He tilted his head to the side, looking at her carefully, then nodded once, accepting her apology. She watched as his face changed, then, sweeping over her features as though evaluating

51

her. "Is it so unbelievable?"

"What?" she asked, grateful that his voice had softened.

"That I'm attracted to you?"

"I suppose there's a first for everything." She scoffed lightly, offering him a small, self-deprecating grin. "But you should make an appointment with your eye doctor when you get home."

His eyes widened in surprise and he tried not to grin back. "Man, you're hard on yourself."

She shrugged. "I've known me for a long time."

He leaned against the flagstones flanking the right side of the fireplace, arms crossed over his chest, facing her. "I haven't. But, you're trim. Athletic. You obviously take care of yourself. You skin looks soft. Heck, it *is* soft. I know because I've touched it. I couldn't resist reaching for your face when I found you." He cocked his head to the side, the warmth of his gaze like a caress. "Your hair's reddish and I like that. Your eyes are blue and I like that, too. I don't know what you think you know about yourself, but if you can't see that you're an attractive woman, the one who needs the eye doctor," he said, "is you."

His words made her heart burst, which had the unfortunate effect of compressing her lungs and making it harder to breathe. "Please don't say such things to me..."

"Why not?"

"I have no idea what to do with them."

"Maybe it's time for you to learn," he suggested, stepping around the coffee table to look at her foot. "How's the ankle?"

"It hurts," she said, her voice still low and breathless.

His hands were on his hips as he flicked a glance to her face. "Can I take a look?"

She nodded and he reached down, lifting her legs gently before sitting down and guiding her feet to his lap. Grace

52

watched him, undone by his words, suddenly very aware that under the blanket she was only wearing panties. She bit her lip, wishing they weren't the serviceable white nylon kind that grandmothers favored the world over, then berated herself for thinking such a forward thing in the first place.

"Whatever's going on in your head, I'm dying to know."

She looked up quickly, knowing her cheeks were pink as she caught sight of his teasing grin and twinkling eyes.

She couldn't help it. She chuckled softly. "I've never sat like this with a man."

"Like how?" he asked, gently unwrapping the bandage from her foot and keeping his eyes down, she suspected, to make her more comfortable.

He'd taken off his snow pants at some point and wore soft, broken-in Levis now, with a plaid flannel shirt rolled up to the elbows. His arms were strong and corded with muscle, blue-ish veins trailing down from his elbow to his wrist. They were thickly covered with springy blonde and white hairs, which Grace eyed with fascination, since Harold's arms had been smooth and elegant, mostly devoid of muscle and hair. Tray's arms made forgotten muscles deep in her body awaken, clenching and relaxing in a way that made her feel weak and wanting.

"Half naked on a couch with my bare foot in his hand."

His fingers stilled and she heard his breath hitch, which did terrible, amazing things to her heart. She held her breath as she watched him clenched his jaw once, twice, before making another slow rotation with the bandage around her ankle.

"You, ah, you never watched TV with your husband? Sitting like this?"

"Harold didn't like TV," she answered.

Tray didn't say anything.

"Did you and Mrs. Bradshaw—?"

"Lena," he supplied softly.

"Lena…?"

"Yeah, we watched TV like this. Now and then. Sure."

"How long were you married?"

"Twenty-six years," he answered. "She died five years ago. You?"

"Thirty-one years. He passed away three."

"Sorry," he murmured.

"Me too," she said. "Cancer?"

He nodded, and the bandage slipped out of his hands onto the floor, leaving her bare foot cradled between his careful palms.

"Your husband?"

"Same." Grace wished that he'd look at her. There was something she needed to know, that she could only know by looking into his eyes as he discussed Lena. She had no right to the information, and frankly, it was probably best if she didn't have it, but she couldn't help herself.

"Tray?" she whispered.

When his blue eyes slammed into hers, she had her answer and her body fairly sighed with relief: He had loved his wife, but he wasn't *in love* with her anymore. He had already let go.

"Are you uncomfortable talking about her?" asked Grace.

"I never have been before."

Did he realize that his hands were gently massaging her toes and foot, easing the tension that had built up quickly as a result of her rigorous exercise and sudden injury? His fingers felt like heaven on her tight muscles and she sighed, leaning back and closing her eyes. "That feels so nice. I'm sorry I make you uncomfortable."

He took a deep breath and sighed, just as she had a moment

54

before. They were silent for several long, strangely charged and yet relaxing moments before he finally answered, "It's not all bad."

"What isn't?" She opened her eyes.

"Making someone uncomfortable." He swallowed. "Been a while since any woman got under my skin so fast, Red."

I'm under his skin? Red? Her blood rushed, sluicing through her veins, making her feel hot and hyper-aware—of him, of herself, of being alone together. It was such a bold and sexy thing to say, of course she had to deflect it, because she couldn't seem to let herself just relax and enjoy this man. "But I'm sure you have a girlfriend, don't you?"

He turned away from her, looking back down at her foot, and again she had her unspoken answer. Yes, he was seeing someone.

"I don't care," she suddenly blurted out.

His hands froze, his head snapped up and his eyes searched her face. "Be careful, Grace."

"No," she answered. "I don't want to be careful."

"What *do* you want?"

Her heart thundered and pleaded. She held his eyes, her mind vaulting forth through time to the *here*, the *present*, the *now*. She somehow managed to smile at Tray, marveling at her bravery.

"I want you to kiss me."

"You sure?"

She dragged her bottom lip into her mouth, holding it between her teeth for a moment before releasing it. "Positive."

His eyes flared, darkening as he nodded at her almost imperceptibly, in agreement and acceptance. He lifted her feet and she bent her knees, giving him space to stand, before straightening her legs on the couch again. He towered over her, staring down at her, his face inscrutable and a little wild, and Grace had the feeling—again—of being utterly naked to him. Her skin flushed and for the first time since she asked him to kiss her, she dropped his eyes.

Tray bent his knees to squat beside her, his hands reaching up to cup her cheeks as he had in the snow, forcing her to look up at him.

"So soft."

She licked her lips, her heartbeat so fast and loud in her ears, she wondered if she'd pass out before she got to feel his lips touch down on hers.

"Say it again, Red," he demanded, his eyes hungry, almost high, as he leaned his face closer to hers—so close she could tell his breathing was fast and uneven because it fanned her lips.

"Kiss me," she murmured, and he leaned forward, touching his lips to hers.

She closed her eyes as he caught her bottom lip between his, pursing lightly, slowly, before releasing it. His lips were warm and soft, but strong too, and for the first time in Grace's life, she felt the marvelous rush of heat that she'd only read about in books or seen acted-out in movies, and she had this satisfied "ah-ha" moment of finally knowing what all the fuss was about.

She leaned forward and placed her hands lightly on his shoulders, her fingers curling just a little to pull him forward, and she heard him drop to his knees beside her, leaning forward, his chest settling upon hers as she lay back and the kiss deepened.

She skimmed her hands up his shoulders to his neck, her fingers trembling from the sensation of his hot skin beneath her sensitive pads. He groaned into her mouth and she arched up to push herself closer to him as he swiped her lips with his tongue and she parted her lips to meet him.

Having been married for decades, it wasn't that Grace hadn't been kissed before, but she'd never experienced this rush of heat—of passion—from kissing Harold. The push and pull of each intense lip lock, the soft sucking sound of his tongue licking hers, the way his thumbs stroked her cheek...it was consuming, almost dangerous, because she almost felt that she would do anything, give anything, be anything, for it to never, ever end.

Chapter 6

Which it did. Too soon.

He leaned back from her suddenly, his chest still pressed against hers, but his face several inches away. Panting lightly, his eyes were wide as they stared at her lips before searching her face.

"Why'd you stop?" she asked, her breasts pushing into the hard expanse of his chest with every shallow breath.

"Because that was…um…" He dropped her eyes, shifting so that he could sit beside her on the couch, and she immediately missed the warmth of his body partially covering hers. Her blanket had slipped a little, uncovering her thighs against the back of the couch, and he righted it, tucking it under her legs and then keeping his hand tucked beneath her as he leaned over her.

"What? What was it?" She couldn't help the ribbon of panic that unfurled through her body, even as she kept her voice calm. *Hadn't he enjoyed it? Oh, God, what if he hadn't?*

He covered his lips with his hand for a moment, staring at her, before clearing his throat. "Intense."

His words made her so happy, she laughed softly. "Don't you kiss all the lonely widows who sprain their ankles in the woods in the middle of a blizzard?"

He shook his head, his cheeks pink as he dropped her eyes,

smiling down at the blanket. "No."

"Never?"

"I've never kissed a guest before five minutes ago," he said softly. "Wasn't appropriate, but I…the way you asked, I couldn't say no."

"I'm glad you didn't." Truth be told, all she wanted was for him to do it again.

"Probably wasn't a good idea, though," he added.

Shoot.

"No?" she asked, hearing the uncertainty in her voice.

He shook his head, removing his hand from under her thigh and scooting back until he rested against the opposite side of the couch facing Grace. He lifted one leg, pressing it flush against hers and kept the other on the floor. In a strange way, it comforted her to still have physical contact with him, even if it wasn't the contact she specifically wanted. It meant that, maybe, he still wanted her.

"Tell me about yourself," she said, anxious to learn more about him, to keep him engaged. "Is Roger your only child?"

He took a deep breath, looking out the window where the snow still fell at a clip. "You want some tea? I could boil some water."

"Sure," she answered. "Thanks." He got up and she instantly missed the warmth of his leg pressed against hers, but wanted to keep him chatting, "You never told me about this place…why isn't it open today?"

He answered her from the kitchen behind her where she heard him opening cabinets and setting mugs on the counter. "It's usually open on the weekends, but if you look in the corner of the room, behind you, by the door, you'll see the hole in the ceiling. Bad storm a few weeks back and a tree fell through the roof. Building isn't up to code until we can get a contractor up to fix it."

She glanced over her shoulder where the corner of the ceiling was covered with a royal blue plastic tarp.

"Is that why there's no electricity?"

"Yep." He set two mugs on the table in front of her, and then headed back to the kitchen where she heard water running. "There's a generator, but I checked when we got here and it's completely covered with snow. I don't even know if it has fuel. I figure we'll be okay with the fire until the snow stops. Plenty of wood."

When he crossed before her again, his hands were covered in long, thick mitts and he was holding an oven rack in one hand and a small, cast iron pot by the handle in the other. He knelt in front of the fire and sectioned off some whitish-orange coals, laid the rack over the coals and gently placed the pot on the grate. Apparently satisfied, he stepped back, taking off the gloves and laying them beside the fireplace on top of the log pile.

To her relief, he headed back to the couch and sat opposite her, lifting his leg again and pressing it against hers. She almost shuddered with relief, reveling in the ease of it, the familiarity.

"To answer your question, no. Roger's one of three. His twin, Derek, is in college out in Colorado. His sister, Tami, is a nurse over in Ithaca. Roger always loved the mountains. Decided to come work at the resort instead of going to college."

"He has a nice personality for the hospitality business," she noted.

He grinned at her. "He doesn't have a mean bone in his body."

"Good parenting, I guess."

"That was all Lena. She was warm as a summer day."

"You must miss her," said Grace, trying to suppress a

ridiculous surge of jealousy.

"I did. Some days, I still do. But I can't live like that."

"The first year was the worst," she said softly, remembering her own first year without Harold.

The sudden realization that she had no one with whom to share news about their children and grandchildren, no one who remembered the little minutiae of their life together. Despite their lack of passion, they'd had a rich life together and she'd turned to Harold with all of her news, her thoughts, her plans. And suddenly he wasn't there to hear her, to nod his head, or chuck her under the chin.

And there were other ways the loss hurt in little unexpected sneak-attacks: Having no steady date for events, no one to take her coat to the coat room and hold the claim check. No one to warm her cold feet in bed and take care of their annual taxes. No one to reach the platter in the top cabinet or roll up the hose when the gardeners forgot to do it.

She had loved Harold, but even more, she'd been accustomed to him. She hadn't really realized all of the quiet ways he'd infiltrated her life until he wasn't around anymore. Losing him was like losing a limb in some ways. And it was challenging to learn how to live without it.

"I thought the second year was worse," said Tray. "Everyone's so concerned about you the first year, and you're in shock. The second year you start to realize all the ways she completed you, and you're left with all of this…incompleteness. Loose ends flapping in the breeze. It's painful to tie them all down. Every time you think you've gotten the last one, another one appears—it's Christmastime and you realize she did all the shopping and wrapping. Or it's time for your annual dental appointment and she's not there to harass you into going." He smiled sadly, his hand dropping to Grace's leg and rubbing distractedly. "By the third year, you can breathe again. You can, I don't know, *stand* it. Bear it."

Grace nodded in sympathy and perfect understanding.

"And then the vultures descend," she added dryly.

He grinned at her. "All those good-looking lonely widows who want to be kissed by a local while they're on vacation."

"I'm not on vacation," she confessed, her cheeks coloring. "My kids sent me to the "Silver Wings" weekend at the lodge."

"How's that going for you, Red?"

She flushed even deeper from the nickname.

"Unexpectedly well," she teased.

He laughed softly, nodding at her. "What about you?"

"What *about* me?"

"Kids?"

"Yes. Two. Well, four. I helped to raised Harold's boys, Henry and Edward. My Addy's thirty-one and her brother, Lloyd, is twenty-nine."

"So you were twelve when you started having children," he deadpanned.

"You're a few years off," she volleyed back, delighted by his compliment.

"Damn fine looking woman, Grace."

"Why, thank you, Tray."

"Damn fine kisser, too."

"And here I thought I could use a little more practice."

His breath caught again in that way she was coming to like so much. It made her feel powerful and sexy, and while Grace wasn't a stranger to power, sexy was a whole new world.

"I don't know if my heart can take it," he said softly, staring back at her.

He might have meant the words as a joke, but his tone was unexpectedly poignant and made her pause, because it was a good point. She'd only known Tray for a handful of hours, but she could tell that he wasn't someone she was going to be able to quickly forget once she was home again. She imagined herself at a hospital benefit, unconsciously scanning the crowd for his face…walking down Fifth Avenue on her way to church and feeling the phantom caress of his warm hands on her cheeks…trying unsuccessfully to fall asleep, night after night, as the memory of his lips claiming hers kept her awake until dawn.

As she resumed her lonely life, she'd know that there was a man living and breathing on the earth who'd made her feel more electric in a few hours than her husband had made her feel in thirty some-odd years. How long would it take to let go of him? Would she *ever* really let go or would he be this unshakable fantasy for the rest of her life?

"What are you thinking?" he asked.

She darted a glance at the fire, where the pot of water hissed and boiled, and finally said something sensible: "That it's time for tea."

***

As they sipped their tea in companionable silence, Grace wondered if Tray was having any of the same thoughts she was.

Granted, they'd only just met one another, but Grace had been alive for almost six decades and she knew that the chemistry she had with him wasn't commonplace. It was…extraordinary.

"So," she said. "You're dating someone? Here at the resort?"

He swung his other leg up on the couch, sinking down a little so that her feet were nestled under his shoulder.

It was late-afternoon and in the past hour or so, it had started darkening outside. When Tray had opened the door of the warming hut, the snow had been piled almost a full foot against the door. She wondered if they were going to have to stay the night and quickly realized that the one and only desperate hope of her heart was that they'd be *forced* to spend the night. She wanted as much time as possible with Tray and she knew that once they returned to the resort, they'd be a guest and an employee again, expected to go their separate ways.

"Sort of," he hedged.

"Who is she?" asked Grace, holding her still warm mug between her hands.

"Why do you want to know this?"

She shrugged because she didn't have a good answer. *Because we're lying on a couch together in the middle of nowhere. Because I like you. Because you like me. Because maybe it'll be easier for me to walk away tomorrow if I think you've got someone else already in your life.*

"Yeah," he said. "Sometimes I go out with Bonnie. She works in the gift shop."

"Ah," murmured Grace, wondering if she was the forty-ish woman she'd spied in the sundry shop this morning. "Is it serious?"

"If it was serious," he said, "I wouldn't have kissed you."

She looked down quickly, bringing her mug to her lips so he wouldn't see how much she liked this answer.

"How about you?"

"I'm supposed to have dinner tonight with Stewart Whitman," she offered.

"Another Silver Winger?"

"Mm-hm."

"Rich?"

"Very."

"Handsome?"

"Quite."

He mumbled it like a curse word. "*Quite.*"

"I know him from home."

"Which is where?"

"Manhattan."

"Of course it is."

"What does that mean?"

"That we couldn't possibly be more different," he said, leaning forward to place his cup on the table, before settling back down. He reached for her foot absently, pulling it onto his chest, stroking and massaging it gently as he pouted.

"That's a big assumption," she said. "I bet we have more in common than you know."

"Like what?" he asked. "You're from Manhattan. I'm from Deer Mountain."

"I'm actually from Connecticut."

He raised an eyebrow and gave her a look that said, *Big difference.*

"You're rich. I'm…comfortable," he grumbled.

"So neither of us have money problems."

He shook his head, but her heart fluttered when his lips tilted up a smidge. "You're well educated. I only have a high school diploma."

"And yet I have no survival skills," she said. "I'd have died out there if you hadn't come along."

"I have a feeling you're made of tougher stuff than you give yourself credit for."

"I love old movies," she said suddenly. "Especially Katharine Hepburn and Spencer Tracy."

He grinned at her. "Me too. And Grace Kelley. You ever see "High Society"? It's one of my favorites."

"Then try "The Philadelphia Story"," she said with a grin. "Same story. And starring Kate."

"I love that one, too," he said. "What else do you do for fun?"

Bad question for Grace since in the past several years Mrs. Harold Edwin Luff III hadn't been a barrel of laughs. She grimaced.

"What's that look for?"

"I'm not very fun."

"Says who?"

She shrugged.

"Give yourself a break and tell me what you like to do," he insisted.

"Read. Especially by a fire."

"Me too," he said, his hands still rubbing her foot.

"Mmm. Anything in the fresh air: Snowshoeing. Cross country skiing. Downhill skiing."

"And in the summer?"

"Anything on a lake," she said. "Swimming, canoeing. We had a sailboat up at Squam Lake in New Hampshire." She grinned nostalgically. "Happy summers."

"There are a couple of terrific lakes here. You were very close to one when you twisted your ankle."

Grace remembered the wide expanse of white she faced while talking to Miss Meyers. "Of course! I'll have to come back to visit it in—in the summertime."

She didn't mean for her words to be suggestive, but they sounded desperate somehow, like she was trying to make a date with him in the future. Her cheeks flamed red, almost painfully, as they sat in silence. But, when she finally found the courage to look into his eyes, he didn't look put off, or like he was embarrassed to be chased by some lonely widow from New York. He stared at her, a sweet smile making his eyes sparkle in the firelight as he held her foot against his chest.

"Will you?"

"Will I what?" she whispered.

"Will you come back, Red?" he asked, holding his breath.

She nodded, offering him a shy smile which answered his own.

Chapter 7

Grace wasn't sure how long they'd been dozing, but when her eyes fluttered open, the cabin was almost dark, but for the rosy glow of the orange and lavender embers in the fireplace. It was cooler too, without the raging flames, but still tucked in her blanket with Tray nestled against her, she was more comfortable than she could ever remember.

Tears pricked her eyes as she realized that she'd probably slept beside Tray for several hours. In the whole of her life, she'd only kissed Harold, only slept next to Harold, and now, suddenly, there was another man's name on each of those lists. She didn't know why it made her sniffle softly, but it did. Maybe because one didn't anticipate so many firsts at fifty-six, let alone two whoppers in one day.

"Grace?"

She propped her head on her elbow to look up at him. "Mmm?"

"You cold?"

"I'm okay," she said, her voice soft and a little ragged from emotion.

"Hey," he said, sitting up and rubbing his eyes. "Hey, now. What's wrong?"

"Nothing," she said. "I'm ridiculous."

He swung his legs over the side of the couch and slid up the slick leather until his hip was pressed up against her belly. His hand landed softly on her upturned cheek.

"You're crying."

She sniffled again, dropping her elbow and laying back. As she stared at the dark rafters on the ceiling, she felt a tear fall from her eye and slide into her hair.

"Remember what you said before? About the second year being the worst?"

"Mm-hm," he murmured, catching the next tear that tried to slip down her cheek, and gently rubbing it away.

"In the third year, you start finding your footing again. In the fourth year…you realize that you don't know anything."

"What do you mean?"

"Before you, I'd only slept beside one man, kissed one man…" Her breath hitched. "I've only ever made love to one man. And now he's gone. Am I expected to pick up where I left off at twenty-two? That's how little experience I have with this. That's how much I've missed."

"No, Grace. No. You haven't missed anything." His voice was tender as he took her hands and pulled her up against him until her chin rested on his shoulder. Wrapping her up in his arms, his strong chest pushed into her soft one as he took a long, deep breath. When he spoke again, his words fell soft and welcome in her ear. "You've lived. You've loved a man and shared his bed. Had children. Maybe grandchildren too. And no, you're not supposed to pick up where you left off the day before you met your husband. You're just supposed to be whoever you are right now. Today."

"I hardly know who that is."

"How great is that?" he asked softly. "To have a second chance to find out who you are. A blank page for the next few decades that you can write as you go along. Who do you want to be, Grace?"

The question reverberated in her ears, too big, too profound to tackle. She'd been a rich little girl, then a college student, then a teacher, then a wife, then a mother, then a grandmother, then a widow. Who was she now? Who did she want to be?

She had no idea.

All she knew, right this minute, was that she wanted more time with Tray. She wanted to talk to him, to listen to his voice, to touch him, to feel him beside her. She'd only known him for a handful of hours, but the only thing written on that blank page was the name Tray.

Leaning into him, she tilted her head to the side, resting her cheek on his shoulder, her lips a breath away from the warm skin of his neck.

"You'll think I'm throwing myself at you," she whispered.

"No, I won't. We're hurtling toward each other," he said softly. "And there's nothing we can do about it."

His words swept through her, making her brave. She arched forward a little, pressing her lips against the throbbing pulse in his throat and listening for the catch of his breath. She felt his lungs, full and frozen, push against her for a long moment, but when her tongue darted out to taste his skin, his breath surged against her ear in a hot rush.

"Grace," he groaned, his voice ragged and rough.

Never having initiated an encounter like this before, she closed her eyes and stopped thinking, just allowing her body do whatever felt good, whatever felt right. Her hands rested on his thighs and she slid them up to his waist, pulling at his loose shirt and slipping her hands inside. His muscles tightened under her fingertips and his breath was shallow, like panting or pain, near her ear. She skimmed her lips to his jaw, under his ear, which she licked and kissed, her tongue flicking across the hot skin that prickled her sensitive lips with a day-old beard.

Suddenly his arms tightened around her and he shifted his face to demand her lips—hungrily, desperately—with a growl of victory as he claimed them. His tongue plunged into her mouth and she arched her back as far as it would go, slamming her body into his as his hands rose to the back of her head, cradling her skull, and holding it in place as he ravaged her mouth.

Grace had never been kissed like this before. She hadn't known that kissing like this was even possible. Her fingers, splayed against the hot, bare skin of his waist, flexed then curled, digging into the firm flesh as he lowered her to the couch, carefully rolling on top of her.

"Is this okay?" he asked roughly, tearing his mouth away from hers for just a moment.

She whimpered in protest, abandoning his waist to palm his cheeks, drawing his mouth down to hers frantically, feeling her need—a terrible, growing, rolling need—for him building in her belly, in her core, all over her body. Her skin longed for his— yearned for every part of him to touch every part of her, and still, somehow, she knew it wouldn't be enough.

She moaned into his mouth as he ran his hands down the sides of her body, cupping her breasts through the thick wool sweater, his thumbs seeking nipples they couldn't possible find through the layers between them.

His tongue slid against hers as his feet dug into the couch and he surged forward gently, into her, against her, his hardness pressing intimately into her softness. Her knees bent to cradle him, her legs sliding up instinctively and then suddenly—

"Oh!" she whimpered. "Ooosh!"

Forgetting about her injury, she'd tried to twist her ankles toward each other around his hips, and managed to wrench the one that had already been twisted. She froze beneath him, pain slicing up her leg unforgivingly as her ankle protested the movement.

He drew his head back, panting, then twisted his neck to look at her foot, resting limply on the back of his leg.

"Sorry," she half-laughed, half-sobbed, all too aware that they were in an incredibly intimate position with each other and wondering what would have happened if her ankle hadn't gotten in the way.

"Not as sorry as I am." He turned back to face her, his smile telegraphing humor and regret. "Are you okay?"

"Unfortunately, I think I should elevate it," she said, dropping her hands from his cheeks, and falling back against the couch in frustrated surrender. She slid her foot back down his leg and he rolled off of her carefully, kneeling beside her on the ground.

"What can I do, Red?"

"Give me an Advil?" she suggested, flicking her glance down to the bulge in his jeans as she sat up. "And a rain check?"

He chuckled softly, standing up and turning away from her to find some Advil in the little office.

"What time was your dinner date?" he called. "With Stew Witless?"

"Stewart Whitman," she said, concealing a grin, loving his little show of jealousy. "Um…eight?"

"It's seven," said Tray. "I still have a little bit of battery left. You should call him and cancel."

"What a shame."

"*Yeah. A real shame,*" Tray mumbled to himself.

"Is it still snowing?" called Grace, trying not to sound *too* hopeful.

"Hard," he said, placing the packet of Advil and his phone

next to her on the couch before turning to tend to the fire. "Call him and cancel. We won't leave until morning."

He said this quietly, with his back to her, and she wondered—just for a moment—if he was lying about the snow. She wondered if it was possible to go, but if he wanted her to stay. It was dark out, so there was no way for her to know for sure unless she hopped over to the door. Maybe the snow *had* already stopped, but he wanted these precious hours alone with her as much as she wanted them with him. The longing in her heart made her question the wisdom of spending more time with him. Did they have any chance of a future after today? No, she thought. Their lives were simply too different. But she hushed her worries. For tonight, just for tonight, she wanted him all to herself, and she hoped that's what he wanted too.

"I'm glad," she murmured, staring at the solid breadth of his back.

"Me too," he said softly, without turning around. "Grace. Aw, Grace, I don't know where the heck this can go, but I'm not ready for it to end yet."

"Me neither," she whispered.

He turned to look at her, his face a mixture of longing and regret, hope and despair. Futility. Surrender. "Will you call him and cancel?"

"Yes." She nodded and his shoulders relaxed as he turned back around.

Reaching for the half-empty root beer, she tore open the Advil and washed them down. Her stomach growled fiercely with the tease of nourishment and she realized that she hadn't eaten since her pastry this morning.

"You hungry?" he asked, then grinned. "Silly question...I'm fairly sure your stomach just woke a few bears from hibernation."

"If I say yes will you show off by heading out into the storm to forage for us?"

He pivoted to look at her, his eyes relaxed now, twinkling with amusement. "Forage? Why, up here in the mountains, ma'am, I prefer to wrestle for my venison."

He laughed, shaking his head at her.

She chuckled right along with him. "You're welcome to a sip of my root beer, but other than that…What do you suggest?"

"Housekeeping cleaned out the kitchen to discourage varmint, but I found some s'mores fixings in the office. When was the last time you had a s'more, Miz Grace?"

"Not since I was a girl."

"Then it's time," said Tray, winking at her. "It's long past time to have one again."

***

As Tray stoked the fire in preparation for s'mores, Grace picked up his phone to call Stewart.

"You've reached The White Deer Inn. This is reservations. How can I help you?"

"Stewart Whitman's room, please," she said.

"My pleasure, ma'am."

And then a moment later, Stewart's voice. "Hello?"

"Stew, it's Grace."

"Grace! How good to hear your voice! I was just about to go downstairs to meet you. Shall I come by your room instead?"

She grimaced at his eager tone. "No. No, Stew, I'm so sorry. I won't be able to have dinner tonight."

"Why not?"

"I had an accident, I'm afraid. The stupidest thing. A skiing mishap—"

"We'll order room service. I'll come to you. Take care of the little patient." He paused. "I have something important that I want to ask you."

Grace looked up to see Tray standing against the flagstones beside the fire, arms folded over his chest, staring at her intently.

"No, Stew, I'm afraid…"

Though he didn't move a muscle, Tray's eyes held hers with a searing intensity.

"Yes, Grace?"

"I'm afraid that's not possible."

She realized then that Tray had been holding his breath, because she heard the short exhalation and watched his chest fill again.

"Not possible? Dinner?"

"Dinner. Your important question. None of it's possible. You're a good man, Stew. But I have thirty or forty years left," she said, holding Tray's eyes as he uncrossed his arms, as his chest filled and emptied again, his skin a godlike golden in the firelight. "And I want to spend them with someone who…"

"Who what, Grace?"

Tray's eyes searched hers in the dim light, and he took a step toward her. Then another, and another.

"Who makes me *feel*," she continued in a breathless whisper.

"For heaven's sake! Feel what?" asked Stewart.

"Everything," she gasped, as Tray dropped to his knees beside her, reaching up to cup her face with his rough, warm hands.

"Well, Grace, I just don't know what to—"

"Good-bye, Stew," she murmured, pressing "End" and letting the phone drop to the couch beside her as Tray's lips slammed into hers.

Chapter 8

Morning light streamed into the room through the bank of windows to the left of the couch, made all the brighter from the snow and ice off which it bounced and sparkled. As Grace's eyes fluttered open, she remembered where she was, and sighed in contentment. Snuggled up against Tray, her back to his front, his arm held her securely against his body under the blankets and her head rested on his arm.

They'd kissed and touched long into the night, holding each other, trading stories about their kids, sharing little tidbits about their lives and giggling like teenagers. After the debacle with her ankle, they hadn't tried to make love again, though Grace knew, if she wasn't injured and they'd had more time, it would have been inevitable.

Time.

And therein lay the problem.

As morning light flooded the little room, Grace realized that they'd run out of time. They had no plans to see one another again once they left the cozy comfort of the cabin and headed back down to the resort. They'd made no promises. They had no plans to be together. They'd spent one passionate night in each other's arms, but Grace was still planning to leave for Manhattan tomorrow morning, and Tray's life, home, work, and family were all here at Deer Mountain.

She twisted in his arms, turning to look at him. She'd taken off his shirt last night as he clutched her to his body, kissing her until she was dizzy and breathless and her ankle didn't hurt anymore. His chest was bare against the thin camisole she'd been wearing under her sweater and turtleneck, and his jeaned legs were entwined with her bare ones.

"Morning, Red," he whispered without opening his eyes.

"How'd you know I was awake?"

"I can feel your breath on my lips," he said softly.

Her face softened as the rest of her body clenched with longing, and suddenly she didn't want to leave the little warming hut. Not ever. For just a moment she wanted to pretend the rest of the world didn't exist. She didn't want to go back to her lonely life in Manhattan—her children, her friends, her fortune, her charities, her penthouse apartment, her needlepoint group.

Who do you want to be, Grace?

Answering that question would be confusing and difficult. If she decided that the new version of herself didn't like her old life, it would require change and compromise. It would mean leaving the comfort zone of her life as Mrs. Harold Edwin Luff III and having the courage to venture forth to find out if there was another version of life waiting for her. A life based on…what exactly? A one-night (almost) stand? A pair of pretty blue eyes? She hadn't been invited to stay, nor had she invited him to come to her. Either option would be insanity after knowing each other for a single day. And Mrs. Harold Edwin Luff III was not crazy, she was sensible. She'd always been sensible.

Who do you want to be?

Her heart thumped painfully as fear coursed through her veins, making her feel skittish and way too self-aware for her own comfort. That fear made her back away from the edge of change, made her retreat to what she knew, to what was unexceptional, but comforting.

You're Mrs. Harold Edwin Luff III, she thought, *just as you've always been. Regardless of the Grace you've been for the last twenty-four hours, you are Mrs. Harold Edwin Luff III in real life. That's what you know. That's who you are.*

"Good morning," she answered crisply.

He opened a blue eye and peeked at her before closing it again. "Yes, it is."

"It's stopped snowing," she said, edging away from him just a little. "I expect we'll leave for the resort soon?"

He tightened his arm around her and drew her closer, nestling his nose in the warm curve of her neck. His voice was scratchy and tender. "No rush."

She clenched her eyes and her jaw, willing herself not to be weak. Tracy Bradshaw simply wasn't enough for her to change her whole life. There wasn't a future with this man, and more precious minutes spent together would only make it harder to leave him.

"We should get going."

His eyes opened and he leaned back, searching her face, suspicion tightening the easiness of his gaze. "Right away?"

"I'm a guest. And you're the ski shop manager. This has been fun, but…"

"Oh." He exhaled heavily, like he'd been sucker punched and the air had been knocked out of him unexpectedly. The warm breath caressed her neck and she forced her face to remain impassive as his hand eased from her hip, sliding away. "Wow. I, uh…I thought…"

She felt like weeping, but was careful not to let it show. "This was…fun."

"Fun. Sure," he said, sitting up and rubbing his hands over his face, which seemed to harden right before her. "But now it's over. Is that right?"

His words felt like a slap, and somewhere inside she knew she deserved it. Somewhere inside she knew she was taking the easy way out...turning her back on the possibility of extraordinary and unknown in exchange for comfortable and familiar.

"Right," she said so softly, she almost couldn't hear her own voice.

He sat up, swinging his legs over the side of the couch and leaned down to pick up his T-shirt off the floor. He pulled it over his head and his flannel shirt soon followed. As he stood up and buttoned it, he looked down at her with a cool expression.

"Well, I guess I'll go dig out the snowmobile so I can get you back down the mountain to the resort. Faster the better, huh, Mrs. Holden?"

"The faster the better," she murmured, swallowing the lump in her throat. From the beginning he'd only called her Grace. She didn't even know he knew her last name.

Her eyes flooded with tears and she looked down so he wouldn't see. She wondered if he'd call Bonnie tonight and tell her about the sad-sack widow he got trapped with—how she was angular and awkward, and had clumsily twisted her ankle and trapped him into babysitting. Grace had absolutely, positively no right to the jealousy and anger she felt, but the ugly fantasy made her voice frosty and imperious.

"Hand me my jeans, please."

He took two steps and grabbed them off the rack in front of the fireplace, then leaned down for her turtleneck and thick, wool sweater, holding them out to her with cold, almost glittering, eyes. "Yes, ma'am. Anything else, ma'am?"

"No," she answered.

"Then I'll hop to it," he said sharply, his voice cracking like a whip when it had been so warm and drowsy just moments before. "Staff at The White Deer Inn aims to please, Mrs. Holden, ma'am."

His face like granite, he shrugged into his parka and let the door to the warming hut slam shut loudly behind him.

Grace's eyes burned and her ankle throbbed as she pulled on her dry, stiff jeans. Her turtleneck and sweater were similarly cold, and she shivered as the chilly fabric pressed against her warm skin. Warm from him.

She'd hurt him.

She'd essentially called him the help and thanked him for "a good time," because whatever was between them terrified her this morning. It was too big to figure out…it was messy and complicated, too new and too unpredictable to take a chance on. How do you mesh the lives of a society widow and a ski shop manager who spend one night together? You don't. Not organically. Not without scary risks and unfamiliar choices, impetuous decisions and the possibility of deep regrets. Not without the censure of her peers and the disapproval of her children.

So, she'd taken the easy way out by alienating him, by humiliating him, by rejecting him, by hurting him so much that he'd hate her and stay away.

"Coward," she hissed, swiping at her eyes.

She swung her legs gingerly over the side of the couch and re-wrapped her ankle, then pulled on her cold, dry socks, one by one. Finally dressed, she stood up, leaning on the couch with her left foot dangling, and hopped over to her ski boots, which Tray had left against the flagstone of the fireplace. Making her stilted way back to the couch, she sat down and carefully pulled them on, wincing as her swollen ankle squeezed itself into the stiff boot.

You had a hand and played it… she thought miserably, thinking about his face as he held out her clothes—the hurt, the confusion, the anger.

She couldn't ignore the quiet whisper of her heart that insisted:

…and lost.

***

Several hours later, she lounged on the couch in her hotel suite, her leg professionally bandaged and resting atop two down-filled pillows, looking out at the same lake she'd stared at yesterday morning before leaving for the rec renter to rent skis.

Before her entire life had changed.

More tears welled in her eyes as she remembered Tray's farewell.

He had picked her up off the couch in the warming hut without a word and deposited her on the back of the snowmobile. Holding onto him as they zigzagged down the hill for thirty minutes was both awkward and heartbreaking as Grace recognized that it would be the last time she was ever so close to him again.

When they arrived at the rec center, she'd quickly dropped her hands, and Tray had carried her into the ski shop without a word before phoning the reception desk and advising that Grace should have an EMT take a look at her ankle.

As they waited in the early morning silence of the empty shop, Grace considered changing her mind and blurting out:

I'm just scared! I've been Mrs. Harold Edwin Luff III for so long, I don't know how to be someone different!

But she didn't. With her chin up and her eyes focused on the door, she said nothing, and was surprised when Tray finally came around the rental desk to stand before her with his hands on his hips. His face was hard, but hurt, his eyes direct but full of disappointment as he addressed her.

"They'll be here in a few minutes and I don't expect we'll see each other again."

"I guess not," said Grace quietly. "Thank you for all you—"

He had interrupted her by holding up his palm like a stop sign. "I asked you last night – Who do you want to be? And I wish to God you'd taken a look at yourself and answered right then and there, because that woman? The woman from last night? She was incredible. I'm positive I met the *real* you last night, and I'm certain she was the woman who fell asleep in my arms.

She was someone I wanted to know, someone I would've tried to hold on to for as long as she would've let me. I would've rearranged my life for her a little or a lot. I would have travelled down to New York to see her, and asked her to come back and see me here. I don't know how it all would've ended up, but I wouldn't have just let her walk away, because I'm not a man who watches someone he wants turn her back and walk away without a fight.

This morning? I don't even know who you are this morning."

He shook his head, pulling his bottom lip into his mouth as he stared at her, his face full of longing and frustration. Finally, when she didn't respond, he rubbed his hand over his mouth and asked her quietly, "Who do you want to be, Grace? The girl you were? The widow you are? Or the woman I had the privilege to meet up on that mountain? Until you figure that out and commit to it, you'll just keep painting yourself and those around you with a broad brush because it's easier. But you'll miss out. I can promise you that."

She stared at him with her lips parted and felt a hot tear roll down her cheek.

He took off his glove and reached forward, swiping the tear away with his thumb.

"I'm sorry," she had whispered, her voice breaking.

"Take care of yourself, Mrs. Holden," he said softly before dropping his hand and turning away.

A moment later the EMT had arrived to check her foot and transport her back to the main lodge, and she hadn't seen or spoken to Tray again.

She had, however, heard from Stewart, almost immediately after she'd settled herself on the couch.

When the phone rang, her heart had leapt, hoping that Tray was calling to check on her, to ask if he could see her, to tell her to stay.

"Hello?" she'd answered breathlessly.

"There's the little patient," said Stewart. "Back from your adventures?"

"Hello, Stew."

"Are you alright, Grace?"

"Of course," she said. "Just a twisted ankle."

"But you had to stay up on the mountain last night? Thank God one of the hotel employees managed to find you in the snow."

"Yes. He was very kind."

"He? Hmm."

"Stew, I'm truly exhausted. Was there something you…?"

"Yes! Yes, of course. You rest. May I order some dinner to be delivered to your room this evening? Six maybe? And swing by to keep you company?"

"Oh, Stew, I—"

"Grace, I—I could make you *feel*," he started impetuously. "I could! I could be more, more—"

"Stewart!"

Her cheeks flamed with embarrassment from Stewart's words and meaning, and reminded her of their short conversation last night when she'd held Tray's eyes, which had burned for her. It made her heart clench to remember.

"Just give me a chance," he begged her. "Please."

"I…I just don't—"

"Dinner, Grace. Just dinner."

"Fine. But in the dining room. And please don't…I mean…," she blew out a breath of exasperation. "Don't expect too much, Stew. We're very old friends."

"And very, very good friends, which, I feel, makes us perfect for each other," he said, then quickly followed up with. "No more, no more. I'll save the rest of my speech for tonight. See you at six?"

"Six," she answered weakly, and replaced the phone to its cradle.

That was a couple of hours ago, and Grace was still sitting in the same spot. Her pot of tea—sent up courtesy of the hotel in a proper silver service—had cooled, and her brain was throbbing as badly as her ankle.

On one hand, she heard Tray's words in her head:

The woman from last night? She was incredible. I'm positive I met the real you last night, and I'm certain she was the woman who fell asleep in my arms. She was someone I wanted to know, someone I would've tried to hold to… I wouldn't have just let her walk away, because I'm not a man who watches someone he wants turn her back and walk away without a fight.

On the other, she heard Stew's:

And very, very good friends, which, I feel, makes us perfect for each other.

Tray's words felt exciting, fierce and passionate, but dangerous and costly.

Stewart's felt sensible, logical and prudent, but too safe, too boring, too much of what she'd already known, and not enough of what she wanted.

What she…wanted.

Who do you want to be, Grace?

Was it possible, she wondered, that the answer she was seeking had nothing to do with Harold, Tray or Stewart, but solely and completely with her?

Pushing herself upright, she stood up on her right leg and hobbled to the sliding glass door, cracking it open and taking a long, deep breath of cold mountain air.

Perhaps there had been a fault in her logic.

Instead of thinking about who she was and what she wanted, she'd only thought of her life in terms of the men in it. And what she realized, standing with her foot dangling and the blank white slate of a pristine snow-covered mountain lake staring back at her, was that she hadn't actually thought of her life in terms of…well, *her*.

"Harold's dead," she said softly. "You're not Mrs. Harold Edwin Luff III anymore."

Whether it was the January cold stinging her eyes, or the fact that in that moment, she finally accepted her husband's death, she wasn't sure, but her eyes watered and burned. After three years, and various stages of grieving, she finally felt it—like glitter being blown away and frosting the landscape before her. Harold would always be with her, but he was also gone.

"You're a grown woman," she continued. "You're not little Grace Holden anymore either."

The coltish, awkward, angular girl she'd been as a bride at

twenty-two was long gone, no matter how poignantly she'd always live on in Grace's psyche. Somewhere along the way, she'd accepted who she was—her athletic body and small breasts. She wasn't scared or ashamed to sleep beside Tray last night. She wasn't an innocent eighteen-year-old who couldn't ask for a kiss. She was a woman who'd shared a man's bed and borne his children. And last night, she'd finally discovered the fierce hunger of passion and known the promise of its requitement.

"Grace Luff," she whispered to the winter wind, marveling at the simplicity of it. "That's who you are. Grace Luff. Luff means love. You deserve grace, and you deserve love."

She was no longer the woman who Stewart had known for over twenty years. She didn't want to chair any more hospital fundraisers or wear pantyhose and wrap dresses to Singles Mixers. She wanted to do more snow shoeing and cross country skiing. She wanted to canoe and swim all summer long, far away from the starched stuffiness of her life in New York. She wanted reading by the fire accompanied by lively discussion, not the polite silence of her needlepoint group. She didn't want lavish parties with unidentifiable hors deouvres, she wanted honest, simple food and a grateful mouth to eat it. She wanted someone she could talk to and laugh with for hours, someone who ordered her around a little and wasn't the least bit intimidated by her money.

"Oh, my," she murmured, bringing her hands to her heart and resting them over her thick, warm wool sweater, one over the over, against her chest.

She didn't want to change for *Tray*. She wanted to change for *herself*. But she knew, beyond any shadow of doubt, the person she wanted to *be*, was someone who would take a chance on *him*.

Grace Holden wouldn't have dreamed a man like Tray Bradshaw could ever look at her with hunger, and Mrs. Harold Edwin Luff III wouldn't have allowed it.

But Grace Luff? The woman she *wanted* to be? The woman she would *become*?

That woman would be grateful for every moment with him. That woman would recognize Tracy's passion for Hepburn in every one of his heated glances. That woman would realize that true chemistry, true heat, true love might only arrive once in a person's life, and yes, it might arrive in the autumn, not the spring. That woman would find the courage to be herself, and not to let something potentially wonderful slip through her fingers.

She wiped away her tears and sniffled, an easy smile spreading across her face as she felt like she was meeting herself for the first time in decades. And in that sparkling white, blank slate, bright, shiny, new, frosted moment, Grace Luff knew that she was finally—*finally*—coming into focus.

Chapter 9

Two weeks later

Since saying good-bye to Grace two weeks ago, Tray hadn't been able to get her out of his head.

Half a dozen times, he'd opened her guest file on the resort computer and looked at her information: her full name (which was Luff, not Holden) and home address, her phone number and e-mail, that she wanted a room on a high floor with a good view and preferred down pillows to foam. That small detail had haunted him for days, and he'd found himself at Target, adding down pillows to his regular purchases of dish soap and softener sheets. Trying them for the first time in his life, he decided he mostly liked them, or at least, he could get used to them.

He'd thought back on their twenty-four hours together over and over again—her clipped coolness when she'd rented the skis, and the relief on her face when he'd rescued her. How light she'd felt in his arms as he carried her, and how she smelled of rose water and fresh air. He grinned as he remembered the way her eyes would flash when he bossed her around, the way she stuck her nose up when she thought he was patronizing her. He'd grimace as he remembered her distrust, the way she perceived that men were just after her for her money, but his face softened when he remembered her apology. And the memory of her lips moving beneath his made his body tighten and his hands would clench as they recalled the softness of her breasts bracketed between them.

Walking by the window of the resort dining room the night they'd returned from the warming hut, he saw her, all dressed up in a silvery white sweater and cream slacks, looking so classy and pretty, it made his heart hurt. He'd decided to try talking to her one last time—he'd ask her to stay for a few more days, and if she said yes, he'd take some vacation time he had coming. They could ski and have dinner, talk more, laugh more, make out more…figure out if there was something real between them and whether or not they wanted to give it a chance.

So his heart had lurched then fallen to see her sitting alone with another man. He couldn't see the face of her dinner companion—though he assumed it was Stewart—but he watched as she covered the man's hand with her own, unable to keep his own heart from clutching at the soft sweetness of her face as her lips moved in conversation. Tray had turned away then, stalked to his car with a hurting heart, and drunk too much bourbon when he got home.

By now, she'd be settled back into her life in Manhattan, he was certain. She'd be organizing those benefits again, and meeting up with her rich lady friends, like Grace Kelley in "High Society"…or Katharine Hepburn in "The Philadelphia Story," both of which Tray had watched more than once over the last two weeks.

After losing Lena, his days had been lonely, of course, but Tray was surprised by how much lonelier they felt now, after meeting Grace. One subsequent date with Bonnie had made it clear their chemistry was almost non-existent when compared to how he'd burned for Grace, and he hadn't asked Bonnie out again.

He'd only known her for a short time, but he missed Grace. He wished things had turned out differently for them.

He wished she'd wanted to give them a chance, but even after his "farewell speech," he'd never heard from her again. Two weeks later, it was time to move on, and yet he knew it was easier thought than done. It might be a little while before he forgot about Grace. What worried him was the prospect that he might not be able to forget about her at all.

Turning his attention to the broken snowshoe in his lap, he used pliers to remove a worn out cleat, and reached for a new one, screwing it into place.

"Hey Dad," said Roger, poking his head into the little office, "lady out here looking for a cross country guide. You want it or should I go?"

Tray sighed. His first reaction was to tell Roger to go, but he'd just given himself a pep talk about moving on, hadn't he? It was time.

"I'll go, son. Give me a minute, huh?"

He put the snow shoe to the side, shucking off his fleece slippers under the desk and reaching for his boots. Pulling them on, he reminded himself to be professional and charming, solicitous and capable. Whoever this woman was, she deserved a first-rate trail guide, and it was up to him to deliver.

He stood up, shrugging into his parka and looking down as he pulled on his gloves and headed through the office door. When he lifted his head, his blue eyes found hers, and seeing her again so unexpectedly knocked the breath from his chest and made his knees weak. He grabbed for the edge of the scuffed countertop between them, staring at Grace Luff like she'd materialized from his longing alone. Unable to regain his composure for several minutes, he drank in the sight of her lightly grey-streaked reddish hair, sparkling blue eyes and mischievous smile.

"Grace," he gasped, completely undone by her sudden appearance.

"Tray," she sighed, her face soft and voice tender as she gazed back at him. "I hear a blizzard's coming. I'd like to rent some skis and arrange for a guide. Do you know of anyone who might be available for a day or two?"

"I might. Grace," he said again, chuckling softly, shaking his head back and forth. "What are you doing here?" Her eyes lost a little luster as he asked this, and he hurried to give context to his question. "I'm so glad to see you! When Roger told me someone needed—I just, I didn't expect it to be...*you*."

She placed her hands on the counter, palms up, and without thinking, he covered them, his fingers curling around hers.

"A good surprise?" she asked, tilting her head to the side.

"The best."

He couldn't help but notice the changes in her: she wore no jewelry and her hair looked stylish, but shorter and more casual. She didn't have that pinched, self-conscious expression on her face that she'd had the first time he met her, and her smiles were easy. Her voice was warmer and more confident, and her eyes sparkled like she didn't want to hold them back anymore.

"You look wonderful," he said.

She grinned even wider. "The mountains agree with me."

"The mountains?" he asked. "But you checked out of the hotel two weeks ago. You went home."

"Hmm," she murmured, her smile fading just a little. "Not exactly. Come sit with me? I'll buy you a hot cocoa."

He looked at Roger who winked at his father. "I've got things covered, Dad. You go on."

Still holding one of Grace's hands, Tray lifted the counter and joined Grace on the other side, letting her pull him over to the little café in the rec center. There, she ordered two hot cocoas, but when she was asked for her room number, she said, "I'm not a guest." and slid two dollars across the counter.

A minute later they sat across from each other at a table in the corner of the quiet café, drinking each other in with the same greediness that they sipped their cocoa.

"You're not a guest," Tray said.

She shook her head. "Nope. I'm a temporary resident."

"What do you mean? You've been *living* here?"

"Sort of," she grinned at him, her cheeks coloring. "I'm renting a house."

"Where?" he asked, feeling so excited, he had to work to keep himself from reaching across the table and grabbing her.

"Bolton Landing," she said, holding his eyes over the top of her cocoa cup as she took a sip.

"That's only twenty minutes from here."

She nodded, her sweet face still smiling at him merrily.

"You mean for two weeks, while I was pining over you like a lovesick fifteen-year-old, you were sleeping up the road?"

Her lips parted in pleasure and her eyes widened in surprise. "Uh-huh."

"Damn, Red." He laughed softly, shaking his head, but then something terrible occurred to him. Last he'd seen her, she was tete-a-tete with Stewart…was it possible they'd decided to buy a house here *together*?

"Tray?" she asked, tilting her head to the side.

"What, um, what made you decide to come back?"

"I never really left. I went home to pack up some things and arrange for my mail to—"

"And um, Stewart?"

"Oh," she said softly, her smile returning, but gentler and more knowing this time. "Are you worried about him?"

"I wouldn't like it if he was here too."

"He's not. He's back in New York. We didn't—I mean, he wasn't who I wanted. He's not the right match for me."

Tray moistened his lips, pressing them together as he stared back at her. "Have any idea who might be?"

"Mm-hm," she said, reaching across the table for his hand. "I have an idea."

He stroked the back of her hand with his fingers, his heart swelling in his chest, beating out a strident rhythm of hope. "Last I heard, you weren't interested in someone who worked at a ski shop."

She nodded, looking down at the table, and he tightened his grip on her hand. Threading her fingers through his, she swallowed once before looking back up at him.

"Can you forgive me for that?" she asked softly. "I was scared. I needed to figure out who I was...what I wanted. That's what I've been doing—reading by the fire and snow shoeing, letting my friends in New York know I was on an extended holiday and wouldn't be available to chair benefits or host book club. I've been spending time up here doing what *I* like to do, and it's like meeting myself all over again. And I know...I *know* it's probably too soon to come looking for you, but I couldn't wait anymore. I needed to see you. I needed to see if there was a chance that you'd—"

Squeezing her fingers, he reached across the small table to cup her cheek with his other hand. His fingers threaded in her hair, he pulled her toward him and captured her lips with his. She palmed his cheek, her fingers brushing against his ear and making him groan softly into her mouth.

He nuzzled her nose, resting his forehead against hers with his eyes closed, relief and surrender almost making him weak. All he wanted—for the foreseeable future—was to spend time getting to know this remarkable, confounding, delectable woman. Did he know exactly what the future held? Of course not. But he'd lay bets that Tracy Bradshaw and Grace Luff were a match made in heaven, and he looked forward to every moment finding out if he was right.

"Yes," he murmured, opening his eyes and watching her tempting lips curve into a smile as his breath kissed her lips. "Whatever you want, the answer is yes."

"Yes," she sighed, drawing back from him finally to fan her pink cheeks.

"Hey, Red," he asked, raising his eyebrows as his glance swept down to her waist and back up. "You know how to use skis?"

He could tell she flashbacked to their first conversation by the way she grinned, nodding her head.

"Yes. But my ankle's just back to normal," she said, then paused. When she continued, her face was just a little more serious, "so we'll need to take it slow."

Pressing his lips to the back of her hand, he understood her meaning. She wasn't just talking about skiing. She was talking about her, and him, and life, and loving. She was giving him a chance at forever, but he was old enough to know that forever was a marathon, not a sprint.

When he caught her blue eyes with his, he smiled at her tenderly and his heart filled when she smiled back.

"Slow sounds fine to me," he said, lacing his fingers through hers, and pulling her to her feet so they could go find some skis and get started on their journey together "We've got all the time in the world."

THE END

(The Blueberry Lane Series #7-10)

Bidding on Brooks
Proposing to Preston
Crazy about Cameron
Campaigning for Christopher

About the Author

Katy Regnery, award-winning and Amazon bestselling author, started her writing career by enrolling in a short story class in January 2012. One year later, she signed her first contract for a winter romance entitled *By Proxy*.

Now exclusively self-published, Katy claims authorship of the multi-titled Blueberry Lane Series which follows the English, Winslow, Rousseau, Story and Ambler families of Philadelphia, the four-book, bestselling *a modern fairytale* series, the standalone novel, *Playing for Love at Deep Haven* and a standalone novella, *Frosted*.

Katy's first modern fairytale romance, *The Vixen and the Vet*, was nominated for a RITA® in 2015, and four of her books: *The Vixen and the Vet* (a modern fairytale), *Never Let You Go* (a modern fairytale), *Falling for Fitz* (The English Brothers #2) and *By Proxy* (Heart of Montana #1) have been #1 genre bestsellers on Amazon.

Katy lives in the relative wilds of northern Fairfield County, Connecticut, where her writing room looks out at the woods, and her husband, two young children, and two dogs create just enough cheerful chaos to remind her that the very best love stories begin at home.

Upcoming (2016) Projects:

Ginger's Heart, a modern fairytale

Jonquils for Jax, The Rousseaus #1 (The Blueberry Lane Series #11)
Marry Me Mad, The Rousseaus #2 (The Blueberry Lane Series #12)
J.C. and the Bijoux Jolie, The Rousseaus #3 (The Blueberry Lane Series #13)

Sign up for Katy's newsletter today: **http://www.katyregnery.com**!

Connect with Katy:

Katy LOVES connecting with her readers and answers every e-mail, message, tweet and post personally!

Made in United States
North Haven, CT
06 January 2024

47132446R00055